"Great speech, doll," Tank said, casually throwing his arm around Melissa. "This time next week I'll be taking out the new president."

"You must be joking! After all that's happened, you don't really think that I want to go out with you?"

"Hey," Tank said. "We've been going together since last fall. Everyone has fights. What's the big deal?"

"Tank, you really are dense! Let go of me, please."

Tank's hold on Melissa tightened. "Nobody puts me down like—" he began.

Melissa looked up to see Lee Hampton beside her.

"Take your hands off my girl, Robertson," Lee said quietly. "You heard the lady."

"Don't tell me what to do!" Tank's tone was outraged, but he let go of Melissa. She stepped back, almost colliding with Janet. Several other students had stopped to stare.

"Melissa!" Janet hissed. "Stop Lee! Tank will murder him!"

Dear Reader:

Thank you for your continuing support of First Loves and your many helpful suggestions. Just as you have requested, we are now including mystery and suspense elements in our books. We are also publishing more stories with the same characters, and have added a new romantic suspense series by Becky Stuart, the Kellogg and Carey Stories. Look for *Journey's End,* the first of these, in October.

And check out our new covers. We have listened to you! From now on you will see that our heroes and heroines will look just like the characters in our books, and more like you and your friends.

Nancy Jackson
Senior Editor
FIRST LOVE FROM SILHOUETTE

FORTUNE'S CHILD
Cheryl Zach

First Love from Silhouette

Published by Silhouette Books New York

America's Publisher of Contemporary Romance

For my mother and father,
who were always there when I needed them,
with my love.

SILHOUETTE BOOKS
300 E. 42nd St., New York, N.Y. 10017

Copyright © 1985 by Cheryl Zach

Distributed by Pocket Books

ISBN: 0-373-06156-0

First Silhouette Books printing September, 1985

10 9 8 7 6 5 4 3 2 1

America's Publisher of Contemporary Romance

Printed in the U.S.A.

RL 6.3, IL age 11 and up

First Loves by Cheryl Zach

The Frog Princess #104
Waiting for Amanda #131

CHERYL ZACH led a Gypsy's life as a child. Her father was career army, and she changed schools ten times in twelve years. Except for two years in Germany, most of this traveling was done in southeastern America. She now lives in California. Before becoming a full-time writer, she taught high-school English.

Chapter One

Melissa could feel all of the eyes in the audience on her. The muscles in her neck tightened and the tension in her shoulders increased as she raised her arms for the last segment of her routine.

But while nervous thoughts raced through her mind, her body moved smoothly in unison with the music's beat. When the music faded, she stood still, and the applause came in waves that pounded against the stage. Trembling, Melissa waited for the curtains to slide across, shutting her away from the noisy audience. Then she stepped back, lowered her arms from her last dramatic pose, and wiped away the drops that beaded her face.

The other girls had been watching from behind the curtain. Some of them were applauding, and a couple frowned at her. Because of her seniority, Melissa had been the last cheerleader candidate to try out, a very enviable position.

"Melissa, you were great!" Janet's familiar voice rang out from the crowd. Melissa smiled toward her friend.

"I wish I could do a cartwheel like that," one of the girls said.

"You really think it would matter?" Tonya's thin, angry voice cut through the girls' murmuring. Melissa braced herself instinctively, but the shrill voice continued. "Miss Popularity herself—it doesn't matter how well she did. Those dumb kids would vote for her for dogcatcher. With her father's money and her mother's hairdresser to help her, who cares how well she does a cartwheel?"

A shocked silence enveloped the stage. Beyond the closed curtains they could all hear the shuffle of feet as students filed out of the auditorium.

"That's not fair!" Janet said. "She was the best cheerleader out there; she did the sharpest routine. You're just jealous, Tonya!"

Tonya tossed her red ponytail. "You should talk, Janet Donnell! You're her best friend."

"The student vote counts only as one-third of the final points," a sophomore, Mindy, spoke quietly. "The faculty committee has the final say."

"So? What does that prove? Miss Goody-Goody makes up to all the teachers, too," Tonya said, her cheeks flushed with anger.

"Tonya!" Mindy protested.

Behind them a couple of girls grinned sheepishly. Melissa turned red.

"Just because you've got two left feet, Tonya Phillips—" Janet began, then paused.

The giggling died. Miss Comstead, the cheerleading sponsor, had come out onto the stage.

"You all did very well, girls. It's a shame you can't all make the cheerleading squad, but you should be proud of your efforts. The list will be posted on the main bulletin board by noon tomorrow." She looked around the stage, as if noticing the tense silence for the first time. "Anything wrong?"

Several girls turned to look at Tonya. Reddening, with her voice more controlled but still resentful, she said, "Some of us don't think it's fair to have to compete against girls who have already been cheerleaders, Miss Comstead."

"It wouldn't be fair to advance them automatically, would it? This seemed the best method," Miss Comstead said.

Tonya's expression was still mutinous. "But they've had all that experience—"

"Yes," Miss Comstead agreed patiently. "But they had to earn the right to gain that experience, just as you hope to do. And they've worked hard for it, believe me. The hours we spent in practice this year!" She rolled her eyes comically, and a few of the girls laughed. The shrill sound of the bell, slightly muffled by the thick curtain, made them start.

"That's the last bell, girls. Better run," the teacher advised.

Several of the girls, who had buses to catch, took her advice literally.

Melissa saw Tonya walk off the stage with another girl. She stared after them and then turned to the door and waited for Janet. "Come on, let's get our books."

Melissa walked beside her friend toward the lockers.

"The first few steps in my routine were pretty shaky," Janet confided as they made their way through the crowded hall. "Did it show?"

"You looked good," Melissa said.

"You'd think after a year I wouldn't be nervous, but it's different when you're out there alone. Maybe the committee won't select me again." Janet continued to worry as they reached the locker they shared and began to pull out books. "I don't think Miss Comstead is too impressed with me."

"Oh, come on. You were great," Melissa assured her again. "You know that the current cheerleaders almost always stay on the squad."

"But I've only been a cheerleader for a year." Janet pushed her thick brown bangs back and sighed. "Now you, two years' experience and co-captain of the squad, *you* don't have to worry."

"Don't speak too soon—it may jinx me." As they went toward the parking lot, she had a curious feeling of being split in two—one part of her walking beside Janet, while her eyes and ears floated overhead, trying to see herself as the rest of the kids did. She noted, from her detached perspective, the students that smiled or waved as she went past, and her own automatic response. What did the kids see—Melissa Abbott, the real person? Or did they see only the blond hair, the expensive skirt and sweater, the cheerleader and student council member that they greeted?

She welcomed the breeze that greeted them as they walked through the double doors.

"Didn't the tennis team have practice today?" Janet asked as she opened the car door and threw her books into the backseat.

"Coach let me off because of the tryouts," Melissa told her. She sat down behind the wheel and dug in her small clutch bag for her car keys.

"Janet"—Melissa turned the key in the ignition—"do you suppose a lot of the kids feel about me the way Tonya does?"

Janet fished through her purse, pulled out her compact, and turned it toward her friend. "Look," she commanded. Melissa, gazing unwillingly into the small mirror, saw her own face frown back at her: the long-lashed blue eyes; the sleek blond hair, cut in a deceptively simple Dutch-girl style that always fell into place no matter how she jumped or twirled; the artfully applied makeup that left her lips and cheeks slightly rosy. Janet snapped the compact shut and dropped it into her bag.

"You're gorgeous," the other girl said, her tone matter-of-fact. "You're going steady with the most popular boy in school. Who wouldn't be jealous? Add to that a rich family—"

"We're not—" Melissa began.

"Well, *I* didn't get a car for *my* birthday," Janet pointed out.

"It was used." Melissa's tone was defensive. "And it's not a fancy sports car, just a small sedan."

They both looked at the lemon-yellow car. Janet shook her head. "Still, most of the kids who have cars had to work for them—cooking hamburgers or dipping ice cream. You got yours with a bow around it—not that that's wrong, mind you," she added quickly.

Melissa frowned.

"Come on, Melissa," Janet said. "Lighten up. Since when do you care what Tonya thinks about you?"

Melissa shrugged, then smiled. "I guess you're right," she said, twisting to peer over her shoulder as she backed the car out of the parking space. Janet was right, she thought. She never cared what people like Tonya thought about her before; she shouldn't let it get to her now.

"I'm so excited about seeing Howie tomorrow night," Janet was saying. "We're really starting to get close."

Melissa grinned. "Yeah, you two make a great couple. Just don't get too close, if you know what I mean."

Janet smacked her in the arm with her pocketbook. "You don't have to worry about me."

When they drove up to Janet's white-frame, two-story house, Janet gathered up her books and purse and turned to get out of the car. "Thanks for the ride; it sure beats taking the bus." She stepped out, then turned toward Melissa. "Oh, I almost forgot. Can I borrow your pink sweater for tomorrow night... unless you had planned to wear it?"

"No, I hadn't," Melissa said. "I'll bring it over in the morning." Melissa couldn't help wondering if even Janet would want to be her friend without fringe benefits. She quickly pushed the thought out of her mind and was angry with herself for thinking it.

"I said," Janet repeated patiently, "has Tank asked you to the spring formal yet?"

"He told me to be sure I had a sexy dress." Melissa made a face. "If you consider that an invitation!"

"You know Tank." Janet grinned. "All he can think about is spring practice."

"That's all he ever has on his mind." Melissa rolled her eyes. *"Football."*

Janet laughed as she slammed the car door shut. Melissa waved and drove away, as Jenna, Janet's little sister, came running out to give her sister a sticky, four-year-old's hug.

Of course Janet was her friend. How could Melissa ever doubt that? As for Tank—Melissa sighed. She couldn't explain even to Janet how the thrill had gone out of her dates with Tank Robertson, Forest Hill's current football star. All the girls at school wanted to go out with Tank; they'd be shocked at Melissa's indifference.

When she pulled into her own driveway, Melissa slowed the car and looked over her home, trying to see it with a stranger's eyes. It was a sprawling tri-level, with a stone chimney rising from a shingled roof. The lawn was carefully landscaped, every shrub perfectly clipped. Most of the time Melissa took her home for granted, but to other people it might be impressive, she concluded reluctantly. She touched the accelerator and drove her car inside the three-car garage.

The house felt empty, but her mother's presence was implicit in every piece of carefully placed furniture, in all the tastefully selected colors. Melissa glanced briefly at the spacious living room, surrounded by a book-lined balcony. From a huge overhead skylight the afternoon sun streamed in, altering and brightening the abstract design on one wall, the Oriental rugs on the floor. She passed through the dining room, with its plum brocade wallpaper, its carefully polished mahogany table, its Louis XV chairs. Through the French doors she could see the deck, with its comfortable lounge chairs, and beyond it a tangle of tall trees already green with spring growth. The view from the deck could make one forget that St. Louis was only a scant thirty minutes away.

Yet despite the attractive surroundings, Melissa felt a sense of unease. She couldn't put her finger on it, but it was there. It had whispered to her in the carpeted hall, spoken to her in the attractively furnished living room, and now was shouting to her in the dining room. What was wrong? There was no doubt in her mind that the mood of the house had changed.

Well, there was no point worrying about that now. It was definitely snack time. She headed for the kitchen.

On the refrigerator door she found a note from her mother:

> Fashion show committee meeting, meat loaf in oven, back by six.
>
> Love,
> Mom

She grabbed an apple, peeked into the oven to make sure the automatic timer was set to start the meal, then took her books upstairs to her bedroom. Sitting down on her bed, she looked over the blue-sprigged wallpaper, the matching drapes, and the bedspread. She had loved this room ever since they had moved in, when she was ten, and her father's fledgling business had begun to take off.

The phone rang, and Melissa reached for it quickly.

"Want to come over and study with me tonight?" Janet asked.

"Not tonight," Melissa answered.

"You sure?" Janet asked.

"Yeah. I'm really tired. I'll just do my homework and then collapse in front of the TV."

"Okay. Don't forget the sweater tomorrow."

"I won't." After she replaced the receiver, Melissa couldn't help wondering which question had motivated Janet's call.

She glanced at the clock, then looked distastefully at the books sprawled across her bed. Her conversation with Janet earlier in the car about Howie popped into her head, and it reminded her to call Tank. But he would be at football practice right now, and anyway, they hardly ever called each other just to talk.

Melissa sat back against the quilted headboard and tried to remember the first time Tank had asked her out—it had been the week of the first big game, when she had just been elected cocaptain of the cheerleading squad. For the first time, she wondered about the coincidence—surely he hadn't cared about her title. Hugging her knees, Melissa opened a textbook and tried to concentrate on her American history, but the horrors of World War II seemed abstract and far away in contrast to her own pressing problems.

When she heard the back door open and close, Melissa was ready for an excuse to leave her homework. She skimmed down the carpeted steps and gave her mother a hug.

"How was your day, dear?" Margaret Abbott was tall, her ash blond hair darker than Melissa's. Her blue silk blouse and linen skirt looked as neat as if she had just put them on, Melissa noticed.

"Fine. We had the cheerleading tryouts this afternoon." Melissa couldn't bring herself to mention the scene with Tonya.

Her mother, who was looking over the day's mail, replied rather absently. "I'm sure you'll be selected; they would hardly drop you after two years on the squad."

"Do you think that's fair?" Melissa asked.

This time her mother focused her gaze on Melissa. "Of course it's fair. The team needs experienced girls. How else can the new girls get the help they need?"

Margaret Abbott moved into the kitchen and began to set the small table in the breakfast area. "Did your father call?" she asked, her tone almost too casual.

"No," Melissa said. "He's probably tied up at the plant." Her mother didn't answer.

They ate dinner quietly, both trying to ignore the unspoken thought that they could not evade.

Not until the last six months had Rob Abbott been absent from home so many evenings.

He's busy, that's all, Melissa thought, trying not to see the lines of tension around her mother's eyes.

"How did the committee meeting go?" she finally thought to ask her mother.

"Much too long, but we did get a lot done. The fashion show is going to be quite successful, I think. We'll have the dress rehearsal next week. Don't forget that I'm counting on you to model."

Melissa nodded.

"Do you have a date with Tank tomorrow night?" her mother asked.

"Yes, we're doubling with Janet and Howie, as usual."

"Movie?"

"Probably." Melissa grinned. "Tank is not very imaginative as far as dates go, and he's addicted to horror movies. This week it's *The Mad Ax Murderer of Sundown Creek*."

Her mother laughed. "Poor you."

Melissa laughed, too. But it wasn't only the thought of another boring horror movie that she wasn't looking forward to. Why did the anticipation of their usual weekly date leave Melissa hoping that Tank would catch the flu?

Chapter Two

Friday morning Melissa remembered to take along the sweater Janet had asked to borrow. When she drove up in front of the white frame house, Janet was nowhere to be seen. Wondering if her friend had overslept, Melissa walked toward the front door, sweater in hand. From inside the house, she could hear a child wailing, and a small terrier danced inside the hall, barking madly.

"Hush, Moppet," Melissa told the dog, which ignored her admonition and continued to bark. "Janet?" She walked inside and called up the stairwell.

"Coming," was the answer. In another minute the wailing subsided and Janet dashed down the steps, two at a time.

"Oh, you brought the sweater. Thanks." Janet took the sweater and tossed it onto a side table. She grabbed her books and they ran for the car.

"We're never going to make the first bell. I'm sorry." Janet's voice was contrite.

"What happened?" Melissa turned her small car carefully into the street and headed for Forest Hill High School.

"Oh, Jenna flushed Tommy's turtle down the toilet. She wanted to see if it would come back up the tank. I had to explain that it doesn't work that way.... Did you get all that history read?"

"Almost."

"Well, I didn't. The textbook is so dry. Thank goodness Rolo makes it all come alive, or I'd never remember it."

"That's for sure," Melissa said. "But I'm not so sure I like it that way. Last week I had to be an S.S. officer. Everyone in class was afraid to talk to me."

The girls made it inside the doorway of 234 just as the tardy bell rang. Melissa headed for her seat.

"Hi, doll." Tank grinned at her from across the aisle. She gave him a quick smile as she slid into her seat.

Tank Robertson had broad shoulders, brown eyes that usually gleamed with mischief, and brown hair cut short to fit comfortably under his football helmet. If, as Melissa often thought, his only concern was with football, at least he was perfectly confident of what he wanted out of life. Right now she almost envied his unconcerned expression, though she would have been willing to bet... "Read the assignment?" she whispered across the aisle.

"You kidding?" Tank continued to grin.

Melissa shook her head. Tank thought that no one would flunk the team's best player, but Melissa suspected that Miss Rolo just might burst his bubble.

"We'll probably have a quiz, you dodo," she told him.

"You worried about Miss Roly-poly?"

"Shh!" she hissed at him, then opened her textbook with an angry flap of its cover. The class became quiet as Miss Rolo began to speak.

Melissa liked this teacher, though she was a tough grader and gave tons of homework. Her pleasant face, framed by curling auburn hair, was quite pretty; it was a shame that Miss Rolo was more than just plump, curving amply beneath her pink flowered dress.

"Take out a clean sheet of paper," the teacher was saying.

Groans rose from the class. Melissa tried to put away her other thoughts and concentrate on answering the questions. Lately it had seemed more difficult to concentrate on her schoolwork.

Melissa had, in her most private musings, dreamed of being class valedictorian ever since her freshman year. She was usually at the top of her class scholastically, and not many of the juniors seemed interested in competing. The thought drew her eyes to a face at the other side of the classroom. Tall and slimly built, his dark hair and eyes revealed his Oriental heritage. He was a newcomer to Forest Hill; he had moved to their suburb just before Christmas, and very quickly Melissa discovered she had a new rival for the position as head of the junior class.

Lee seemed to feel her gaze, because he turned his head slightly and met her eyes. Melissa stared at him for a long moment, but she could not tell if he resented her interest, welcomed it, or simply couldn't care less. Flustered, she looked down at her textbook.

When Miss Rolo handed back last week's tests, Melissa was stunned by her grade. She had studied so hard—but that was the morning her parents had had a loud argument over breakfast, and the echoes of the unusual quarreling had seemed to block out her hours of study.

Melissa stuck the embarrassing paper into her notebook. She could make up for one bad grade, surely. Yet she was not prepared for the next blow.

At the end of the class, the teacher passed back their last research assignment. Homework in this class was assigned on a weekly basis, and Melissa had done her work carefully.

But the grade read: Forty-seven. Failing. Melissa looked up to see Tank receive his paper, then quickly turn it over on his desk.

"Melissa," Miss Rolo said quietly, "I'd like to talk to you and Tank after class."

After the other students had filed out of class, Melissa followed Tank up to the front desk.

"You do know my rules about doing your own work?" Miss Rolo looked at them steadily, and Melissa felt her cheeks burn. "These discussion questions are designed to make you think. I don't want someone else's thoughts. The answers on these two papers were identical. Therefore, the grade of ninety-four has been split between you."

Melissa thought there was definite reproach in the teacher's blue eyes. Her embarrassment turned to anger.

"If you would like to make up some of your lost points, you may take an extra-credit assignment from the file in the back of the room. Remember that it must be turned in in three days."

Melissa hurried to pick up an assignment card, then ran to catch up with the ball player.

"Darn it, Tank! You told me you wanted to check a couple of answers. I never said you could copy the whole paper!"

Tank shrugged. "I didn't think she'd spot it— old Roly-poly has real eagle's eyes."

"That's not the point. I feel as though I'd been the one who cheated!"

"Don't get so ticked." Tank looked down at her from his superior height and grinned. "It's no big deal."

"Forty-seven is a big deal!"

"With your smarts, you'll make it up in no time. I'm the one who ought to worry."

"That's true." Melissa gave him a pointed glance. "But you never do."

Tank just shrugged again. "Old Roly-poly gives too many assignments, anyhow. I've got practice every day. What does she expect?"

"Don't call her that. She's going to hear you one day," Melissa warned, but he only grinned.

"Why not?"

"Because people have feelings, you knot-head," Melissa said. The sound of the second bell made her turn.

"See you tonight, " Tank called after her, his voice as lazily cheerful as ever.

Melissa, running toward her next class, didn't bother to answer.

When she looked for Janet before lunch and didn't find her at their usual rendezvous, Melissa remembered the list of cheerleaders for the first time. Walking quickly toward the front hall, she saw a crowd of girls surrounding the bulletin board, blocking the sheet of paper from her view. It took several nerve-wracking minutes before Melissa could edge close enough to read the names.

Janet had made it, and Stephanie, and two new girls, Annette, a junior, and Mindy, a sopho-more. Melissa's heart began to beat faster as she scanned the names, until at last she saw "Melissa Abbott" at the very bottom. Not until that instant did Melissa realize how much she had taken for granted her readmission to the squad.

She took a deep breath to steady herself. She had made it. Then, forgetting the crowd around her, Melissa looked over the list again. Tonya's name was not there.

Melissa tried to feel badly for the other girl, but the memory of Tonya's harsh words at the tryouts made it difficult. She turned to push her way out of the crowd and was startled to see Tonya's flushed face only a few feet from her own.

"I guess you're happy," the girl said, her voice sharp and high-pitched. "Miss Popularity comes through again."

"I'm sorry you didn't make it, Tonya," Melissa said, trying to make her words sound sincere. It was hard to feel cordial toward a person who glared at her with such open animosity.

"I'll just bet you are." The other girl walked away.

Hot words rose inside Melissa, but she hesitated to voice them. An angry scene would make them both look foolish.

Melissa walked to lunch. At the cafeteria entrance, she found Janet, who grabbed her in an impulsive hug.

"We made it!" she shrieked. "Aren't you happy?"

"Relieved is more like it," Melissa answered. "My name was all the way on the bottom of the list!"

The girls found a table toward the back of the cafeteria and put their books down while they went to get some food. "Did you notice that Tonya didn't make the squad?" Melissa asked her friend, trying to sound casual.

Janet gave Melissa a long long. "Oh, Melissa, you're not starting in on that again, are you?"

"Well, I saw her in the hall and she once again informed me that I am a spoiled rich kid who gets everything I want." Their conversation was momentarily interrupted by some girls who wanted to congratulate them for making the cheerleading squad. They made their way back to the table with their trays of food.

"Anyway," Melissa complained, picking up right where she left off, "I'm sick and tired of being thought of as just another pretty girl who has everything. I want more out of life than just getting by on my looks." There was a pause. "My dream is to be class valedictorian."

Janet stopped eating and looked squarely at her friend. "To be what?"

"You heard me."

"Melissa, is there anything you don't want? I mean, why can't you be satisfied with what you are? Half the school would die to be you, or at least look like you. I know I would."

"Can't you understand? I want to be liked and known for *who* I am, not for what I look like."

"Well, I hardly think it's that serious. I mean, you're not exactly the beauty queen of the world." Melissa was silent. "Listen," Janet continued, "I think you're going to have some pretty tough competition against the new kid, Lee something-or-other.''

Melissa thought about the quiet, aloof boy. Yes, there was certainly going to be competition there. "But he's not my only problem," Melissa said, and she continued to tell Janet the story of her two low grades in history until the bell rang and cut their conversation short.

The afternoon seemed very long. Putting away her books, Melissa thought of the extra assignment in history and made a face. She still had one essay to write in lit class, too; she hadn't needed the extra work. Oh, well, I'll just have to get it all done, she thought.

Melissa had gotten excused from her last-period study hall in order to hit a few tennis balls before practice began. Smacking the balls across the net helped relieve some of the tension she had been feeling lately, and soon she had forgotten everything except hitting the balls.

Breathless and out of balls to hit, Melissa wiped her forehead and looked up. In the distance, she saw Lee Hampton, bending down to pick up one of the wayward balls she had hit over the fence.

"Thanks," she said, walking over to the edge of the court, near where Lee was standing. He threw the ball to her and she smiled. "Going for a run?'' Melissa asked, noticing his sweat pants and sneakers.

''Yes,'' he answered quickly. ''I must go now.'' He looked intently into Melissa's eyes and held her gaze for a moment. Then he turned and ran down to the field.

Melissa shivered. His gaze held something strange, but what was it? Her thoughts were interrupted when the rest of the tennis team came out, and the rest of her afternoon was spent without any thoughts other than improving her tennis strokes.

Later, as she stood in the shower at home while the warm water needled her shoulders, Melissa thought without much enthusiasm of the evening's plans. The same old boring thing with the same old boring Tank. Earlier, when she'd asked him if they could do something new, he'd said, ''Sure, doll, we'll see a new movie.'' Melissa had to laugh out loud at that one.

She selected a skirt and sweater from her closet, and was ready by seven. It was a quarter past the hour when Tank finally drove up, and she walked out to the driveway.

Janet and Howie were already in the backseat of the sedan, and they greeted her cheerfully. Melissa slipped into the front seat, and Tank gunned the motor. ''Hi, doll.'' He grinned. She grimaced.

The movie was the usual blend of Hollywood horror and special effects, with liberal amounts of gore. Melissa shut her eyes in the worst spots and was glad to see the credits roll by on the big screen. Then, as always, they went out for a quick hamburger so that the foursome had half an hour to spend at Lookout Point.

This was the part of every date that Melissa dreaded. For thirty minutes or so, until the girls' curfew forced them all toward home, her partner in romance suddenly turned into an octopus.

That night, when she had removed Tank's wandering hand from her knee for the third time, Tank, breathing as heavily as if he had run ten laps around the field, protested, "Oh, come on, Lissa."

"You know I can't stand that name," Melissa told him, feeling irritable and not caring if it showed. "I think it's time to go home. Don't you think so, Janet?"

Janet was usually quick to respond to Melissa's tacit pleas for aid, but that night there was no reply.

"Janet?" Melissa looked into the backseat and watched her friend unwind from a lingering kiss. "Don't you think it's time to go?"

"Already?" Janet sighed absently.

"Already!" Melissa glared at her.

"Okay," Janet growled. "It's getting late."

Melissa turned around and folded her arms in front of her. There was more silence in the back. She wanted to see what was going on but didn't dare turn around. Instead, she turned to glare at Tank.

Tank's expression seemed rebellious, but under the force of Melissa's unrelenting stare, he finally reached to turn the key.

They dropped Janet off first, then continued toward Melissa's house. The front light was on, and Melissa was unwilling to linger on the step.

"Why not one more kiss?" Tank insisted.

"It's past twelve. I'm going to get into trouble, Tank." She turned away from his arms and dug into her purse for her house key. "I've got to go in."

"Oh, all right," he grumbled. "See you Monday."

"Right." She let herself into the silent house, trying to make as little noise as possible. But she had hardly reached the staircase before her mother called, "Is that you, Melissa?"

"Yes, Mom." As clearly as if she'd been told, Melissa knew that her father was not yet home. And it was past midnight. She waited for the expected scolding from her mother, but her mother remained silent, she was too preoccupied with her own.

She made her way up the steps and into her room, shutting the bedroom door barely in time to jump at the ring of her phone.

"Hello?" She spoke anxiously into the receiver.

"It's just me," Janet's voice answered.

"Do you know what time it is?" Melissa was thankful that she had her own private line; maybe her mother hadn't heard the ring.

"Well, I was afraid you were mad. I'm sorry we were late. Did you get into trouble?"

"It's okay," Melissa told her. She had almost forgotten the familiar tussle in the parked car.

"It's just—when Howie kisses me, it's hard to remember the time, or anything. You know?"

Melissa, who felt mainly annoyance at Tank's heavyhanded romancing, sighed. "Sure." She didn't know at all; she wondered now if there might be something wrong with her. But Melissa wasn't ready to confess such an unnatural reaction, even to her best friend.

"Talk to you tomorrow," Janet said.

"Okay."

The phone clicked, and Melissa replaced the receiver. Pulling off her clothes, she tossed them toward the chair at the side of the room and crawled into bed. That night she wanted to forget everything—Tank, with his wandering hands; her low grade in history; the envious Tonya; her dad's late hours.

She dreamed about tennis practice. Lee Hampton had just thrown her the tennis ball. His expression was tantalizingly enigmatic. "Tell me your secret," she begged, but he shook his head and walked away.

Chapter Three

Saturday Melissa slept late. When she finally pried herself out of bed, she pulled on some jeans and a T-shirt, made her bed, then went downstairs. As she passed her parents' bedroom, the door slightly ajar, she wondered what time her father had come home, if there had been an argument, and if they had made up.

In the kitchen her mother was standing with her back to the door, pouring coffee into a mug. When she turned, Melissa was surprised to see her usually immaculate mother still in a robe, her hair uncombed. She had deep circles under her eyes.

Melissa poured herself a glass of juice. "Isn't Dad up yet?" she asked as she inspected the cereal boxes in the pantry.

Her mother didn't answer. Melissa filled a bowl with cereal and went to the refrigerator for milk. "He's not gone already?" she asked, her voice sharp.

Margaret Abbott nodded.

"But I didn't even see him," Melissa complained.

Her mother turned away abruptly. "I'm going out to the deck," she told Melissa. "It's too cool in here."

Melissa, left alone in the kitchen, ate a few bites of cereal, but the food seemed tasteless, and she soon pushed it aside. She rinsed her bowl and put it in the dishwasher. About to follow her mother onto the deck, she paused at the sight of a small framed snapshot. She picked up the photo and carried it outside.

Margaret Abbott was sitting on a chaise longue, her face toward the sun, her puffy eyes protected by dark glasses.

"When was this taken?" Melissa asked.

Her mother smiled at the old picture. "Don't you remember? No," she said flatly, answering her own question. "You would have been too young. That was the day we paid off the first bank loan, the one your dad used to buy the original plant.''

"It wasn't very big then, was it?'' Melissa said, thinking of the small factory where her father's company manufactured parts for lawn mowers.

"Just two rundown buildings and about a dozen workers. There are over a hundred employees now.''

"You worked with him, didn't you?'' Melissa asked. "In the beginning?''

"Oh, yes.''

"What did you do?''

"Everything. Typed his letters—composed half of them. Helped keep the books, talked to customers, argued with creditors.''

"Sounds as if you had fun,'' Melissa said. "Why did you stop?''

Her mother looked at her in surprise. Melissa, still intent on the image of her father and mother working happily together, saw the answer unaided. "It was because of me, wasn't it?'' Melissa felt a wave of guilt flow over her. "Did you hate me for that—getting in the way, I mean?''

Her mother set down her coffee mug so quickly that some of the liquid sloshed over the rim. "Of course not!'' she said. "We—your father and I—were both thrilled when you were born. I wanted to stay home with you, Melissa. I didn't want to miss those first years. Then, later, when you were in school, the business had grown so much that there didn't seem to be a need for me any longer."

"Dad has always worked hard, hasn't he?" Melissa asked.

Margaret Abbott nodded. "He deserves his success; there's no doubting that."

But, Melissa thought, the plant is doing well. Why isn't he ever at home? What's wrong?

"Do you think the business means more to him than we do?" she asked, very low.

Her mother put one hand to her temple briefly, then said, "Of course not." But her voice was subdued.

For a moment they were both silent. Then her mother rose slowly and turned back toward the kitchen. "I think I'm going to lie down awhile," she told Melissa.

"I'll be over at Janet's," Melissa said.

She shut the back door carefully and checked to see if her tennis racket was still in the back of her car. Maybe Janet would play a few games.

As she pulled out of the garage, Melissa noted absently the faint tire marks left by the oil she had picked up coming through the new road construction yesterday. There was a lot of work being done on this side of town. They would have to scrub the garage floor again. Then her gaze slid over to the side where her father's sedan always sat. The floor was clean.

Melissa sat motionless in her small car and felt a smothering sensation, as if she could not breathe. He had not been home at all last night. No wonder her mother had lain awake all night, waiting. How could he do this?

She didn't know what to think. As she drove toward Janet's subdivision, she tried to sort it all out.

Perhaps her father had gone away on a business trip; that happened sometimes. But surely her mother would have known, wouldn't she? As Melissa parked her car in Janet's driveway, she remembered suddenly that her father had hired a new secretary only a few months ago. Melissa had seen the woman only once or twice, on quick trips to her dad's office, but as far as she could recall the woman was quite young, obviously not very experienced. Perhaps her father had left a message and Miss—that was it, Miss Lelman— had forgotten to call.

It was the most sensible explanation that Melissa could think of. When she knocked at the door, Janet called, "Come in."

Melissa found her best friend sitting at a round kitchen table with her little brother and sister, lots of paper, and two bottles of glue. Janet looked harassed, and Jenna had more glue on herself than did the project under construction.

"What's up?" Janet asked.

"Thought I'd see if you wanted to play some tennis," Melissa said.

Janet shook her head. "Can't," she said. "Tommy's got a science project due Monday and he's just begun."

"So I see," Melissa said, looking at Tommy, who was trying to read a fragment of comics upside down. "What's it supposed to be?"

"A model of a beaver dam…. Jenna!" Janet spoke sharply. "Stop eating the glue. Sorry, Melissa."

"That's okay. Can I use your phone while I'm here?"

"Sure." Janet looked a little surprised, but she waved toward the back of the house. "No one's in the den."

"Thanks." Melissa couldn't bear to wait till she got home to check out her theory; besides, she didn't want to risk having her mother overhear her phone call. Not knowing what was happening was making her a nervous wreck.

She dialed the usual number, and the voice that answered seemed familiar. "Abbott Manufacturing. May I help you?"

"Mrs. Tibbot, is that you? This is Melissa."

"Why, hello, dear. What can I do for you?"

"Is my father in his office?"

There was a slight pause. Then the woman answered slowly, "No, Melissa, I'm sure he isn't."

"Is he on the floor of the plant?"

"I don't think he's here today, Melissa." The answer was firm this time. "We have only a small shift working on Saturday just now."

"Miss Lelman isn't there, I guess?" Melissa persisted, still wondering if a message could have gone astray.

A long silence followed this time, and the voice on the other end sounded somewhat strained. "She doesn't work Saturdays, Melissa. Can I do anything for you?"

Tell me where my father is! Melissa thought. "I guess not," she said. "Thanks, anyhow."

She hung up the phone and walked back to the kitchen, where sounds of noisy debate could be heard.

"Tommy, beaver mounds don't have doors on the top. The entrance is under the water," Janet was saying. She gave Melissa a grin.

"You've got glue on your nose," Melissa told her.

"But we don't have any water," eight-year-old Tommy objected. "Hey, can we put some water in it?"

"No," Janet told him. "Water would dissolve the cardboard."

"Where's your mother?" Melissa asked.

"She had to work at the P.T.A. bake sale. She left grumbling; she hates bake sales. And I got stuck with the beavers." Janet dabbed futilely at her nose.

"Jenna's eating the glue again," Melissa warned.

"Oh, rats." Janet snatched at the glue bottle, and her little sister began to wail.

"What's all the fuss about?" Mr. Donnell came through the doorway, his arms full of bags of groceries.

"Daddy!" Jenna shrieked. She made a run for his short, stout figure and clutched at his trousers legs, leaving sticky handprints.

All the Donnells began to talk at once. Melissa, watching them, saw Mr. Donnell place the groceries on the counter, then bend down to console his youngest, ignoring the damage to his trousers. Melissa felt a lump rise in her throat and a dangerous prickling behind her eyelids. She took advantage of the bedlam to slip away into the hall.

Leaning against the wall, she wiped her eyes and swallowed hard. She had her face under control before Janet came after her.

"Melissa, sorry about all of this. Maybe we can play tennis tomorrow."

"Sure," Melissa said. "I'd better get back home."

"I don't blame you." Her friend grinned. "My crazy family would drive anyone away."

Then she stared at Melissa's face. "What'd I say?"

"Nothing," Melissa managed to say. "Talk to you tomorrow." She almost ran for her car.

When Melissa reached home, a note was attached to the refrigerator.

> Dad called, away on business. I've gone to lunch with Katie.
>
>   Love,
>   Mom

So that's where he was, Melissa thought. But why did she still feel this empty ache inside.

Melissa was glad to see Monday come and be able to forget her troubles in the familiar routine at school.

When she saw Tank, as she and Janet walked inside the double doors, she gave him an unusually warm smile.

"Hi, doll." Tank's greeting was as breezy as usual. "Tell you what, you're going to have the election for May Queen in the bag."

"What?" Melissa tried to turn her thoughts back to school and the upcoming spring formal.

"You've been in the court for the last two years. And I've got the whole team ready to vote for you. You know what they say—as the team votes, so votes the school."

Melissa laughed. "I think you just made that up." She didn't mind that he stepped closer and put one arm around her shoulders. It felt good having somebody so close to her.

"So what?" Tank grinned. "As long as you win."

"Does it matter?" Melissa asked him.

"Matter?" Tank sounded shocked. "The May Queen is the prettiest girl at Forest Hill High. You know that. Of course it matters."

Melissa, shrugging off his encircling arm, turned to stare at him. "Do you think I'm pretty, Tank?"

"Dumb question!"

"But that's not the most important thing, is it? I mean, would you still go out with me if I weren't pretty at all?" Her tone was serious, and she felt a shock of dismay when Tank looked away from her anxious gaze.

"How am I supposed to answer that?" he complained. "You're always pretty—I can't imagine you any other way. I like a girl who cares about how she looks, you know?"

"Only the best for Tank Robertson," Janet said from Tank's other side as she rummaged through the locker. Her tone had an edge that startled Melissa. Tank gave the shorter girl a quick frown.

"Shut up, chubby!" he snapped.

"Tank!" Melissa said.

Janet drew her slightly stout frame up as tall as possible. "Sure, Rudolph," she said sweetly, then walked away.

Tank, who allowed no one to use his real name, glared and took a step after her.

"Tank, that was rude." Melissa grabbed his arm.

He snorted. "I just tell it like it is," he said. "Come down to my locker with me."

Melissa shook her head. "I'll see you in class." She hurried after her friend and caught up with her just outside the history classroom. Janet grinned a little sheepishly at her.

"I'm really sorry about what Tank just said," Melissa apologized. "But what did you mean with your comment?"

Janet shrugged. "Oh, Howie told me that Tank boasted to the whole locker room that he only dates the most *gorgeous* girls." She made a face. "Maybe I'm just jealous. Forget it."

"Isn't that funny," Melissa said, staring thoughtfully ahead of her. "Tank told me that

Howie was bragging about how he only goes out with the ugliest girls around.''

Janet looked at her for a minute, and then both girls broke out into laughter. "You think it's funny," Janet said with a lightened voice. "Just be glad you look the way you do." Melissa grimaced slightly and walked into class.

Tank wandered into class just after the tardy bell.

"That's your third tardy, Mr. Robertson," Miss Rolo told him.

Tank, confident that he could talk his way out of detention with football practice as an excuse, only shrugged. He took his seat and glanced toward Melissa, but she refused to meet his eyes. Rebuffed, he simply turned to whisper to the redhead on his other side.

Melissa opened her textbook. For a moment she felt as if someone was staring at her. She looked at Tank, but he was still talking to the redhead. Her gaze drifted to the far side of the room. Had Lee Hampton met her eyes? When he turned away, she wasn't sure if she had imagined that moment of contact.

In English, Melissa remembered for the first time that she had an essay due, and had not written it. She couldn't believe that she had forgotten about it. Her hopes for being number one in the class were fading.

When she met Janet for lunch, she was frantic. "I've got to do this English paper by the end of the day. I can't believe I forgot all about it." She whipped out her English notebook and began writing.

"Melissa, valedictorians do not forget to write English papers," Janet said. "Where is your mind lately?"

Melissa gave her friend a sour look. "I don't know. I just know I have to get this done, okay?"

"Sorry." Janet took out a book and started reading. "Oh, I picked up the nomination forms for the student council election. You need fifty signatures to qualify for the ballot."

Melissa looked up from her notebook. "What?"

"You *are* running for student council president, remember?" Janet gave her a disgusted look. "I said I'd be your campaign manager, and we need to get started. John Barton already has his posters up."

"Oh, I just don't know. I'm so behind in all my schoolwork, I barely have any time. As soon as I catch up, we'll get started."

"Melissa, is something wrong?" Janet asked.

"Why do you ask?" Melissa looked down at her book and continued writing.

"You seem to be in a strange mood lately. I mean, forgetting to do your homework and stuff. That's not like you. Are you mad at me?"

"Why should I be mad at you? Are you crazy?"

"If it's what I said about Tank, don't worry about it. I think he likes you."

"This"—Melissa blew rudely into her straw—"to Tank Robertson!"

Both girls laughed, and Melissa closed her book and concentrated on discussing campaign strategies with her friend. After all, she was only trying to help, and it stopped her, at least termporarily, from asking any more questions. Melissa didn't want anybody to know what was happening at home, not even her best friend.

When lunch period ended, Melissa went upstairs to chemistry. In this class at least she was not only up to date on her assignments, but she was even somewhat ahead. Checking her lab notebook, she had an idea.

"Mr. Clayton," she said, "I've completed this unit. Could I go to the library and do some research?"

"I suppose so," the teacher answered, watching two boys who were dangerously juggling some test tubes. "Put those down!" he yelled. To Melissa, he said, "Write a hall pass and I'll sign it."

In a few minutes Melissa was on her way to the library. With the extra-credit assignment in history not done, and the English essay she had done little work on at lunch still not finished, she had plenty to do. She deliberately chose a study carrel in the back, hoping that its high sides would hide her from any passing acquaintance who wanted to talk, so that she could work undisturbed.

Yet, when she settled down with several thick books, Melissa found that she couldn't concentrate. She kept remembering the undefined trouble at home. She gritted her teeth and tried to follow the long sentences of the history book, but a new sound made her stiffen. She would have recognized that shrill voice anywhere.

"Look—I did this poster myself."

"Are you really going to campaign for John? I thought you didn't like him," another feminine voice asked.

"You bet. Why should that stuck-up Melissa Abbott get it? She reminds me of a girl I read about once in a book—she was called 'fortune's fair-haired child.'" Tonya's tone held so much bitterness that Melissa shivered.

"Why—because she's blond?" The other voice asked.

"No, stupid—because she's got everything!"

"Well, she may not have Tank Robertson much longer. I hear he's been flirting with that pretty new girl who moved here from Atlanta. I don't think Melissa knows, though."

"That's not all she doesn't know." Tonya's voice was chilly with a malevolent triumph. "Her dad's running around town with his new secretary, who's not much older than us, my mother says. She saw them at a restaurant downtown Saturday night. My mother says he's making a real fool of himself."

Melissa felt as if she'd been suddenly drenched in ice water. Cold seeped through her, and her breathing seemed to stop. It's not true! she thought. But she remembered her mother's swollen eyes, and a dreadful certainty replaced her first instinctive disbelief.

The voices continued, but Melissa tried not to listen. If they would just go away without seeing her—she couldn't bear for Tonya to know how badly the girl had hurt her. *Go away!* she prayed.

But, instead, the voices came closer. Melissa bent over her books, trying to present the picture of a student too absorbed to notice a passing conversation. She felt rather than saw the two girls come into view, and heard one of them gasp and hurry to change the subject.

"He's probably—oh!" The shorter girl muttered. "Now, where was that book you wanted?"

But Tonya was made of sterner stuff. "Look who's here, the great lady herself."

Melissa began to gather up her books. She was in no shape to trade insults with Tonya, and she could just pretend for one more minute that she had not heard those awful remarks— But Tonya refused to let her off so lightly. "What do you think about your father's latest romance?" she asked, as if they were discussing a television serial. "Or does that sort of thing happen all the time in your neighborhood?"

Melissa felt her cheeks flame, and her throat tightened beyond speech. She wanted to hurl hateful words at Tonya, but she didn't trust her voice. Her tears were close; she could feel them behind her lids. She stumbled toward the main part of the library, colliding abruptly with a boy who rose out of another study carrel—a boy whose presence she had not suspected.

He held her by the upper arm, steadying her. Melissa tried to pull away.

"Please," she murmured. "I can't—let me go."

"No." He spoke so firmly that she looked up at him, despite her numbing despair. It was Lee Hampton who stood so close, who held her arm in such a firm grip.

"What she said—the whole library must have heard." Melissa's voice was heavy with pain.

"Yes," Lee agreed. "And if you walk out looking like that, they'll believe it's true, instead of dismissing it as another random jibe by a jealous girl. Get hold of yourself."

"I can't," Melissa whispered. She was trembling, but he did not release his hold.

She had never heard him speak so firmly, or at such length. He was so quiet in class, responding so inaudibly even to the teacher's questions, that she had never heard his voice properly before. He spoke perfect English, without any accent, yet with a hint of the cadence of another culture. At another time it would have fascinated her, but now Melissa noted it only vaguely, in a distant part of her mind.

"Yes, you can," he was saying.

"But—" Melissa felt the dampness of tears against her lashes.

"You can—and you must." His voice was hard. "When I first came to this country, the children taunted me, called me names. But I never let them see that they hurt me. That would allow them to win. You can't give in, Melissa."

"How?" She looked into the deep darkness of his eyes.

"Draw into yourself. You can deal with the hurt later."

Under his intent gaze, Melissa stood up, swallowed the aching lump in her throat, and wiped the dampness from her lashes.

"That's better," Lee told her. He squeezed her arm before he released her, and the small gesture helped Melissa walk steadily out into the open floor space.

The tables were crowded with students. Some of them glanced curiously at Melissa. She wondered how much of the angry diatribe they had heard, how much Tonya might have said before.

But, with Lee's admonitions still in her mind, she walked steadily across the carpeted floor, her expression serene. This time the split image of herself that had dogged her for days seemed useful; the hurting could be kept inside her until she was alone.

Melissa drew a deep breath when she reached the hallway. If she walked slowly enough, she could stretch out the remaining time in the class period. Pausing by the water fountain, she splashed cool water against her face and wondered about Lee. How had he become so adept at dealing with pain?

Chapter Four

Melissa lingered in the hallway until she heard the shrill sound of the bell. The noise of people talking, moving—the click of leather soles against the smooth floor—brought with it a surge of panic. Melissa felt her perilously gained composure slipping away, and she turned, looking for a way to escape.

Just behind her a classroom door opened, and people began to spill into the hall. Melissa grabbed the nearest doorknob and pulled, stepping recklessly inside.

She found herself in a small, windowless office, with two desks, only one of which was occupied. Miss Rolo looked up from a pile of papers, her expression surprised.

"Melissa, what's the matter?" she asked. Her voice was light and pleasant.

"Melissa?"

Melissa tried to answer, but her throat was aching again, and she felt one tear slide down her cheek, and then another. She put up one hand, trying to hide her face.

"Do you want to talk about it?" Taking Melissa by the shoulder, she gently pushed her toward a chair.

Melissa shook her head.

"Woud you like a drink of water?"

Melissa nodded. Miss Rolo opened her desk drawer and took out a paper cup. She walked out into the hall. As the door swung open, Melissa heard the babble of conversation and the shuffle of students filing down the hallway. Then the door shut and the noise faded. In the quiet and solitude, Melissa could relax a little.

In a minute Miss Rolo came back with water from the drinking fountain. Melissa accepted the paper cup, thankful that the teacher wasn't asking a lot of questions.

"Feeling better?"

Melissa nodded and wiped off her cheeks. She opened her purse to dig out her compact and lip gloss. The familiar motions steadied her.

"Thank you," she said. "I'd better go to class." She still dreaded the inquisitive faces of her classmates, but she would have to face them sometime.

"If I can do anything for you, Melissa, do tell me." The teacher's voice was concerned and kind. Melissa managed to smile. She dropped the empty paper cup into a trashcan and went back into the hall. The crowd had thinned out; it was nearly time for the tardy bell. Melissa hurried to her next class.

In French III the class was preparing to watch a film on French artists. Melissa sank into her accustomed seat and sighed with relief when the lights were switched off. Not until the end of the hour did she realize that someone was watching her. Lee Hampton was sitting at the back of the room; it was his gaze she felt again.

What a loner he is, Melissa thought. He even sat by himself, separated by two desks from the nearest student. He moved through the school like a shadow, quiet-spoken, perfectly behaved, making excellent grades, but seeming not to need companions. She envied his apparent self-sufficiency.

When the class ended, Melissa lingered at her desk. She didn't realize that she had been hoping that Lee would speak to her again until he paused by her desk.

"You okay?" he asked.

Melissa, standing with her books in her arms, nodded. "How do you do it?"

He raised his dark, level brows, his expression difficult to read.

"You don't seem to need other people, or care what they think about you," Melissa continued.

He shrugged. "Why should I?"

"Have you been hurt that badly?" Melissa blurted out, then wished she could recall her impulsive words. But it was too late. Lee drew back slightly.

"I'm sorry," Melissa stammered. "It's none of my business, is it?"

"No," Lee agreed, and walked away.

So much for Lee, the lone wolf. She headed toward the girls' locker room. Her last-class period was free; in the fall and winter she worked with the other cheerleaders; in the spring she devoted the hour to tennis practice.

Coming into the gym, Melissa saw Tank, already dressed for the football field, standing by the door. He had apparently been waiting for her, because when he saw her, he moved quickly to intercept her.

"What's the idea, Lissa?" he demanded.

"What?" Melissa had almost been pleased; now she felt deflated all over again.

"I heard you've been hanging around that Hampton guy—that he had his arm around you in the library."

"What?"

"A Chink, yet. Is it true?"

"Tank, will you ever learn not to call people—"

"Oh, forget that. Is it true?"

"Anyone who saw me talking to Lee Hampton must have looked quickly," Melissa said crossly, wondering if Tonya was trying to create more trouble.

"Then, it is true?" Tank looked like an indignant bull, clenching his jaw until his neck seemed to swell. "You're trying to cozy up to—"

"Of course not," Melissa said. "I can talk to anyone I want to, Tank Robertson! I don't have to spend my life in a test tube just because we're going out."

"I've got my reputation to think of." Tank's tone was belligerent. "My girl doesn't hang around with just anyone, you know? Especially not some foreigner."

"He's not foreign." Melissa's anger grew to irrational heights. "If you had anything between your ears besides a hunk of pigskin, you wouldn't judge people by how they look. All you do is label people—foreign, fat, pretty."

"Don't let this May Queen bit go to your head, Lissa," Tank warned. "You're not the only pretty girl in school, you know. You think I can't take my pick?"

Remembering the comments in the library, Melissa answered softly. "I understand you're already looking."

Tank looked defensive. "Why not?"

"Why not, indeed," Melissa said. "Happy window shopping, Tank." She walked toward the locker room, ignoring Tank's puzzled stare.

Tennis practice seemed to go on forever. Melissa was anxious to get home, yet when she finally parked her car in the garage and let herself into the kitchen, the house was still empty. She frowned at the note on the refrigerator. Another meeting.

It had never bothered her before to find no one at home. Now she wanted to scream and rant at somebody.

It was almost five when she heard a car pull into the driveway. Waiting for the inner door to open, Melissa saw her mother enter, looking more weary than usual.

"Hello, darling," she said.

"When is Dad coming home?"

The abruptness of the question seemed to leave her mother at a loss for words. She took off the silk scarf that had been knotted about her neck. She avoided her daughter's eyes. "What?"

"Mother, you heard what I said. When is Dad coming home?" Melissa discovered she was shouting; she had never yelled at her mother so fiercely. Some part of her was shocked at her own conduct, but her frustration was overwhelming.

"Melissa, I don't know."

"You don't *know?* Where is he?"

"He's staying at an apartment in town." Her mother's voice was very low. Melissa had to strain to distinguish the words.

"He's left home?"

"He—he wants some time to think about things, he said."

"Are you getting a divorce?" Melissa was almost whispering now. This nightmare was too dreadful to be voiced.

"I—we—I don't know yet, Melissa."

"Why didn't anyone tell me anything?" Melissa wailed, her voice rising again. "For heaven's sake, Mother, how could he just leave like that, without telling me? I haven't even seen him since the beginning of last week."

"Perhaps he doesn't know what to say to you, Melissa," her mother began.

"Why are *you* making excuses for him?" Melissa interrupted. She turned and ran up to her room, shutting the door with unnecessary vigor.

How could this be happening? It was like a bad dream, but she couldn't wake up. What would all the kids at school say? How Tonya would love this latest development!

She curled herself on the bed like a child, hugging a stuffed dog to her. How could her father do this? Allowing himself to be seen by the whole community escorting a woman half his age—the sheer embarrassment of it! And he hadn't even called! Didn't he wonder how Melissa felt? Didn't he care?

After some time, she heard her mother call, "Melissa, dinner's ready."

Melissa went downstairs obediently. With lowered eyes she sat down at the table. In strained silence she and her mother ate dinner.

"The rehearsal for the club fashion show is tomorrow night, Melissa," her mother told her as she began to clear the table.

"You don't really expect me to go walk around the stage so that everyone can stare, after what's happened?" she demanded.

Margaret Abbott stiffened. "Melissa, we have to keep on with our lives—" she began in a determinedly reasonable tone.

"I won't." Melissa's voice quavered. "I'm not modeling in the show. Just count me out."

"Melissa—"

Melissa didn't wait to hear any more. She ran upstairs again, grabbed the stuffed dog, and tossed it hard against the wall.

She was behaving childishly and she knew it, but she couldn't seem to stop. She almost wished her mother had yelled at her, instead of looking at her with so much concern.

She couldn't stand this house any longer, she decided. To sit here and stare uselessly at her school books would make her even more frantic than she already was. She picked up her notebook and purse and went downstairs.

"I'm going to the library," she told her mother, who was sitting at the kitchen table. "I need to do some research."

"Be home by ten," her mother said tonelessly.

"I will," Melissa promised. A part of her wanted to walk across the hall and hug her mother, yet something held her back. She felt angry toward her, though she couldn't explain exactly why. Perhaps it was the half-formed feeling that her mother should have somehow prevented this awful thing from happening. She could hardly wait to get into the car and drive through the deepening twilight the few blocks to the library.

Once in the library, she checked out a few history books and sat down at a corner table intending to concentrate on her history assignment.

Instead, she found herself watching various readers come and go. An elderly woman was leafing through the file cards. Two little girls were giggling in the children's section.

Melissa saw a tall boy enter. As she idly watched him check in his books, she recognized Lee Hampton. His sleek black hair gleamed under the fluorescent lights when he walked past her. Had he seen her? She couldn't be sure. He set his book bag down on an unoccupied table toward the back of the room and shrugged off his jacket before sitting down. After a moment's hesitation, she gathered up her belongings and walked over to him.

"Hi," she said softly.

Startled, he looked up. "Oh, hi, Melissa." His tone was cool.

Somewhat nonplussed, Melissa asked, "What are you working on?"

"A special project for chemistry. I want to win a college scholarship."

"Do you need one?" Melissa asked before she realized how tactless the question was.

"My father—my adopted father, I mean—is a doctor. He can afford to send me to college, but I would rather not be a burden to him," Lee answered. He glanced down again at his books as if only courtesy had kept him from ignoring her altogether.

"Lee," Melissa said quickly, "my church youth group is having a picnic Sunday afternoon. Would you like to come?"

It was an impulsive invitation, yet now that the words were out, she didn't regret them.

Lee glanced once more at Melissa. His gaze was serious.

"I'm sorry. I have to wash my parents' car. Thanks, anyhow."

Melissa was stunned. She had never been rejected with such an excuse. He had to *wash a car,* for heaven's sake? Was he so turned off by her that this was the only excuse he could muster? Or were his parents ogres who insisted that he study or work every waking minute? It just didn't bear thinking about! "That's okay," she said with a feigned smile. "I'll see you around." She hoped he couldn't see her crimson face as she turned to leave the library.

Once she got to the car, she tossed her books in the backseat and retrieved her keys from her jeans pocket. The encounter with Lee had temporarily taken her mind away from her other problems, but driving home these all came back to her. She walked inside the house with listless steps and managed to slip upstairs without disturbing her mother.

She was upstairs brushing her teeth when she felt a light touch on her shoulder. "Good night,

Melissa," her mother said. Again, Melissa had the impulse to throw her arms around her mother, but her curious anger persisted and prevented her from doing so. She pretended not to know that her mother had lingered a moment and was still watching her.

After her mother had finally left, Melissa collapsed into bed. But she spent a restless night. She knew that when families split up there was often a shortage of money; now this began to worry her. How much did her father earn? She hadn't a clue. And her mother hadn't worked since the birth of Melissa. Another thought followed with sickening logic. Would they have to give up their house? All week she'd felt smothered and unhappy at home, but now it dawned on her just how much she loved her home, and what a terrible fate it would be to leave it. Where would they go? How would they manage?

It was a hollow-eyed, exhausted Melissa who dragged herself out of bed the following morning. After her shower, she dressed slowly and went downstairs. She stared at the rooms as she passed as though seeing them for the first time.

Her mother was already in the kitchen. Melissa could smell the coffee and cooking sausage.

"Like some French toast?" her mother asked as Melissa came through the door.

"Yes, please." Melissa slid into a chair after pouring a glass of juice for herself from the refrigerator.

Resisting all her mother's attempts at conversation, she mumbled a few replies and hurried through her breakfast. When she had finished, she stacked her dishes in the dishwasher and headed for the door. "Gotta run," she said, ignoring her mother's good-bye and last-minute admonitions. She knew she was behaving badly, but she couldn't help it. Her one desire was to get out of the house.

Janet was waiting for her in front of her house. They got into the car and headed for school. When they drove into the school lot, Janet said, "Just what *is* wrong with you?"

"Nothing," Melissa answered, avoiding her friend's gaze.

"You haven't said a word the whole way. Something bothering you?"

"I'm okay," Melissa said. She couldn't bear to have anyone, especially her friends, know just how imperfect her family had become. She remembered Tonya's taunt: "fortune's fair-haired child." How ironic it seemed now!

"Well, if you don't want to tell me—" Janet's tone was stiff. She picked up her books and they both walked toward the building.

Just inside the entry, several large posters had been taped to the wall. One said: VOTE FOR JOHN BARTON—BRAINS, NOT BEAUTY. The next proclaimed: THE STUDENT COUNCIL PRESIDENCY IS NOT A BEAUTY CONTEST; VOTE FOR JOHN BARTON!

"Would you look at that!" Janet gasped. "Talk about underhanded—I'm going to talk to Mr. Cochran, the student council advisor. That's going too far."

Melissa read the signs silently. How much more of this could she take?

"That's Tonya's doing!" Janet fumed. "You take my word for it. John's not smart enough to think of it."

The first bell rang and the girls headed for class.

The morning passed slowly for Melissa. Tank ignored her during history. When she caught his eye, his look was cold. Had her angry words yesterday left an impression? Melissa pushed the thought aside.

She was in algebra class, spending the last few minutes of the period working on the homework assignment, when the beeper on the wall sounded. When the teacher picked up the handset and spoke a few words, he called her name.

"Melissa?"

"Yes?"

"You're wanted in the office."

Melissa closed her notebook and hurried out of the room. As she approached the main office, she saw several students waiting to talk to the secretary. Not until she entered did she see who the tall man with sandy brown hair was.

Chapter Five

"Daddy!"

Ron Abbott smiled at his daughter. "Hi, Melly," he said. "Thought I'd take you out to lunch. How about it?"

If he looked a bit ill at ease, Melissa was too thrilled to pay much attention. "I need to put away my books," she said.

"Just throw them in the backseat of my car. I promised the principal I wouldn't make you late for your next class."

They walked out into the afternoon sunshine. "Where are we going?" she asked, getting into her father's big sedan.

"How about Justin's?"

"Sure," Melissa said. "Sounds great." This informal steak house had for years been a favorite of the Abbott family.

Neither spoke during the short drive. Mr. Abbott seemed unable to break the silence, and Melissa was content just to be with her father again. It seemed an eternity since he had moved out of the house.

When they reached the restaurant and had been shown to a small booth in the back, Melissa and her father gave their order to the waitress.

Alone once more, Melissa looked shyly up at her father. How handsome he is! she thought. "It was nice of you to think of taking me to lunch," she told him.

"Your mother called and said you were upset because I hadn't talked to you myself," he said.

Melissa's smile faded. So taking her out hadn't been his idea, after all! And she had actually believed he had wanted to see her! She could feel painful tears of hurt spring to her eyes.

"She was right, of course," her father was saying. "I should have talked to you earlier, Melissa." He paused and ran one hand through his sandy hair. "I don't know how to start."

"Why did you leave?" Melissa asked.

He picked up his fork and used it to draw creases in the cloth napkin. "Melissa, it's difficult to explain..."

"I guess so." Melissa tried to keep her voice level, though she could taste angry tears in the back of her throat. "I thought you and Mom were happy."

"We were, Melly," her dad said. "But things change, people change. You wake up one morning and it's not the same. It's as if you've blinked your eyes and two-thirds of your life is gone. The people around you look like strangers, and you're not sure who you are, or where you want to be. Sometimes you have to try to find out."

"Are you going to get a divorce?"

"I—I don't know yet, Melly," he said. "But I want you to know that it doesn't involve you. I still love you, and your mother loves you, and we don't want you to be upset." He gave her the same one-sided smile that she had known all her life, the smile she associated with happy, ordinary days of raking the lawn, playing tennis, swimming in the lake.

"I'm not *involved?*" she cried. Her voice wobbled and almost broke. "You don't want me to be upset? For crying out loud, you're not that stupid! How can you sit there and say that to me?"

Her voice was rising, and at the corner of her vision, Melissa knew that a woman at another table had turned to stare. She tried to get hold of herself.

Her father's expression had gone from one of surprise to rising anger. "As much as we love you, Melissa, the whole world wasn't created for your benefit. You have to think about other people."

"And you do?" Melissa asked.

His angry gaze dropped, and Melissa looked away. The waitress came with their lunch. Melissa's steak sandwich looked tender and savory, but the lump in her throat wouldn't allow her to swallow. She tried to keep up the pretense of eating, but it was hard.

Soon her father was glancing at his watch, saying, with a quick look at her stormy expression, "We'd better get you back to school."

The drive back was as silent as the first one had been, but for a different reason. Now it was intensely painful for Melissa to be in the company of her father. Yet when she'd collected her books and got out of the car, she wanted to say, "When will I see you again?" But pride held her back. Why should she have to ask? She waited for her father to say something, something loving, but his only parting remark was a quick, "Take care, Melissa."

Melissa walked inside the building and turned down the hall, hoping to find Janet. At the door to the cafeteria, a tall, broad form almost passed her before she realized who it was.

"Tank!" she said. Melissa had forgotten her irritation; their quarrel seemed to have taken place long ago. Tank was part of her life, and with so much changing, it seemed important to hold on to as much of the familiar pattern as possible.

"Uh, hi, Melissa," he said.

"Have you got time to talk?" Melissa asked, wondering if she dared to tell him about how terrible her life had become.

"Well..." Tank hesitated and seemed positively relieved when the bell broke through the noise from the lunchroom. "Got to go, Melissa."

"Okay," Melissa agreed, disappointment heavy inside her. "What are we doing Friday night, Tank?"

"Well..." There was a moment of silence. Then as people began to stream through the doors and the force of the crowd pushed them apart, Tank yelled, "I'm sort of tied up on Friday, Melissa. See you." He disappeared into the mass of students.

Melissa felt as if he'd hit her. A passing student bumped into her, and she had to struggle to maintain her footing. Flustered, she got herself out of the doorway and away from the crowd, then tried to pull herself together.

She had never been stood up in her life. She found it difficult to believe. Rejected by two boys in two days, and her own father didn't even care if he saw her! It was all too much.

Melissa walked aimlessly down the hall. She stared blindly at the glass door of the counselor's office, and her reflection stared back. The girl in the glass looked pale and heavy-eyed, but she was pretty, no doubt about it, well dressed, and slim.

What had happened? Melissa wondered. She was still all she had been a few months before, and yet her life was in a shambles.

She was late to chemistry. To add to her miseries, Dr. Webb gave the students a pop quiz and she failed it dismally. Looking over the blanks on her paper, Melissa realized that her grades, unless something changed quickly, would be beyond recall. Her dream of being valedictorian was gone and another part of her life was dissolving before her eyes.

Janet was at their locker when Melissa arrived to put in her books before tennis practice.

"What's the matter?" Janet asked. "You look about as cheerful as a rat in a trap."

"Tank broke our date for Friday," Melissa told her, too dejected to evade the question.

"What?" Janet looked astonished, then indignant. "He can't do that! Howie doesn't have a car."

Melissa laid her cheek against the cool metal and laughed helplessly.

"I'm sorry to interfere with your social schedule, Miss Donnell," she said.

"Well." Janet looked offended. "You can laugh. Any boy in school would jump at the chance to go out with you. Me—that's a different story. Howie's the only boy who's really liked me. And I like him, darn it."

Janet's image of the situation was so far from the truth that Melissa laughed again, and her friend glared at her.

"I'll try not to jeopardize your transportation, dear friend." The remark was supposed to sound funny; instead, the bitterness in it startled even Melissa, and Janet drew back. Yet Melissa couldn't seem to stop herself. "Why don't you make out a schedule of when you'd like to go out? Maybe include which of my clothes you'd like to wear."

Even as they were said, Melissa regretted the words. But it was too late. Janet, pale beneath her freckles, gasped. "If you don't like me borrowing your clothes, Melissa Abbott, you should have said so! Believe me, I won't bother you again!"

She tugged at her textbooks, almost sending the whole pile cascading to the floor. "Don't wait for me after school," she said as she left. "I'll take the bus. I wouldn't want to inconvenience you."

Melissa was left with a locker full of sliding books and five minutes to make tennis practice.

It came as no surprise that she missed all the balls. She faulted at serve after serve, until the coach came up behind her and said, "What's wrong, Melissa?"

"My whole life," she said.

He laughed and walked on.

Melissa, who hadn't meant to be funny, gritted her teeth and tried another serve, watching it land far to the right of the center line. Her partner yelled, "Come on, Melissa!"

"You serve, I'll return," Melissa called, adding to herself, "if I can hit the ball."

The drive home seemed very quiet without Janet. And the house was empty again. A note on the refrigerator said:

Cold cuts inside; home by ten.

The fashion show rehearsal was that night, Melissa remembered, the one she had refused to take part in. She knew perfectly well that her mother had been working on this project for months, and that the proceeds would go to a local children's clinic. It was a worthy cause, and her mother had the right to be involved. Yet, in a totally irrational part of her mind, Melissa felt rejected. No one wanted her; no one seemed to be available when she needed them.

Fortune's fair-haired child, indeed.

She was too depressed to be hungry. She nibbled on a pear, then went up to soak in a hot tub, deciding to wash her hair in the morning. She was in bed staring at the ceiling when she heard her mother's car in the driveway.

Melissa switched off the bedside lamp and frowned into the darkness. She heard her mother come upstairs, hesitate outside the door, then push it open gently.

"Melissa?"

Melissa, her eyes tightly closed, didn't answer. In a moment her mother stepped back outside, pulling the door closed behind her, and Melissa heard her go back down the staircase.

Melissa opened her eyes. Why had she done that? She lay awake a long time but did not hear her mother come to bed.

When Melissa awoke the next morning, she discovered that she had forgotten to set her alarm, and it was past seven. Grumbling to herself, she pulled on a robe and stumbled downstairs. The kitchen was empty. No smell of crisp French toast or grilled sausage or scrambled eggs. Not even the fragrant aroma of her mother's coffee.

Melissa felt distinctly aggrieved. Her mother was always up early. Was she angry at Melissa?

Then Melissa saw the wineglass sitting in the sink, and she went over to lift the clear glass and sniff it in disbelief. Her mother seldom drank, and never to excess.

She slammed the glass down so hard that the fragile stem snapped; shards of glass flew across the counter. It seemed a fitting metaphor for her life. What else could happen to her family? It wasn't fair.

She had no appetite for breakfast. She climbed the staircase slowly and went into the bathroom.

Staring at herself in the mirror, she almost laughed. If the kids at school could see her now! The pretty girl, the girl from the perfect home, whom no problem could touch. A lot they knew!

Pretty? She examined her reflection. Her unwashed hair was dull and limp; there were dark shadows under her eyes. Like most fair-haired people, Melissa had light brows and lashes, and without makeup she looked pale and listless. If they could see her now...

The thought made Melissa's brows rise. Why not? Let the whole school see that Melissa Abbott could be just as plain—even as ugly—as anyone else. Let them see that "her ladyship" was just another peon, and the special aura that Tonya and the rest seemed to envy so ardently was only a mirage of their own making.

Melissa washed her face and brushed her teeth, but she did not open her makeup drawer, and she did nothing to her hair except pull a comb through the lank strands.

Then she went to her bedroom, pulled from the back of her closet a ragged pair of jeans and a khaki shirt that she had bought back when military garb had been the current fad. Its drab color was so unbecoming she had seldom worn it.

She pulled on the garments quickly, then looked at herself in the mirror. Perfect!

Her mother would have protested against the wearing of such an outfit, but her mother wasn't up to see it. Melissa's resolve hardened. Tossing her head defiantly, she headed downstairs. She had decided that she would not stop for Janet. What was the point? It had been quite obvious the day before that their friendship was cooling.

When she reached the high school, Melissa walked through the halls. She was surprised at how few students met her eyes; she seemed almost invisible. In spite of her intentions, the sensation was both shocking and unpleasant. It wasn't that they seemed to be avoiding her; they just didn't see her. Was it true, then, that only her appearance mattered?

She saw Tank near the history classroom and hastened her steps so that she could pass him, curious to see what his reaction would be.

But he walked straight past her, his eyes brushing over her face without any sign of recognition.

Melissa stopped and leaned against the wall, feeling a little dizzy. It was true. Melissa Abbott was only a mirror image—take away the makeup and the clothes and there was nothing left.

She walked slowly into the classroom, dreading the students' reaction. Hurrying to her desk, she sat down.

Why, she thought, had she ever thought it exciting to go out with a boy like Tank? This was the first time she looked less than picture perfect, and he didn't even know she was there.

Was this how her mother felt—rejected for a younger, maybe prettier, woman? She had been so full of her own anguish that she hadn't stopped to wonder how her mother must be hurting.

Miss Rolo, handing out papers, paused beside Melissa's desk. "You don't look well, Melissa," she said. "Would you like to go to the nurse's office?"

"No, thank you," Melissa muttered, embarrassed by her concern.

"Is it one of those days?" the girl behind her whispered to Melissa. "I have some aspirin."

Melissa shook her head. This was dreadful. All she had wanted to prove was that she could be like everyone else—not special, not perfect. She looked over to Janet's desk, but it was empty. Maybe she had a doctor's appointment. She wanted to look at Lee, but after his rejection the other night, she refused to allow her eyes to betray her interest. She tried to listen to the teacher.

The rest of the morning was no better. In English class, Mrs. Montclair said, "Melissa, you don't look like yourself today. Anything wrong?"

Melissa, staring at the term "dramatic irony" on the blackboard, wanted to laugh. She shook her head. This was ridiculous. She was supposed to be unattractive, not sick.

It was not their sympathy she wanted, Melissa thought, aware of the glances of some of her classmates, but their understanding. She wanted them to see that Melissa Abbott was an ordinary person, who could be dull, who could be unhappy. It was some understanding of the real Melissa she had hoped for, in order to crack the illusion of the perfect prom queen.

How could she ever just be herself—just Melissa?

She became aware that the teacher had asked her a question, and she hadn't even heard. Melissa flushed. "May I go downstairs to the nurse's office?"

At the teacher's nod, Melissa grabbed her books and fled. In the hall, she hesitated. After putting her books into her locker, she couldn't think of what to do. She didn't want to have to answer the nurse's questions, yet she didn't want to go back to class, either.

Melissa laid her cheek against the cool metal door of her locker and felt an unhappiness that was worse than sickness. She was trapped by her own image. No one would allow her to be anything but fortune's child—happy and pretty and confident. No one wanted to know the real Melissa, who could be as confused, as miserable, as anyone else. She felt like the storybook Alice, trapped behind a mirror in a world where things were not what they seemed. And no one cared.

Footsteps sounded in the hall, and Melissa stiffened. A teacher would wonder why she was out of class. But it was a tall boy with a weird hairstyle. Melissa tried to remember his name. Jack, Jack something. He was in none of her classes, so she seldom saw him, but she remembered that he had been suspended several times.

She turned toward her locker to hide her face, but he paused just behind her.

"What's up, Melissa?"

"Nothing much." She wished he would walk on, but he lingered, watching her.

"You don't look like your usual shining self," he said. "Feeling down, Melissa?"

"What if I am?" Melissa saw him reach inside his jacket and extend his hand.

"I can show you how to feel better." His voice held a sly note of challenge.

Melissa stared at his outstretched hand, at the small scarlet capsules that lay cradled in his palm—so sinister and so seductive.

She felt her scalp crawl with distaste, yet in his offer lay the promise of escape. Despite herself, she put out her hand, allowed him to drop the pills into her palm, marveling at how light they were.

And an iron-hard grip seized her wrist and twisted, so that the bits of color dropped to the floor, to be ground into dirty bits of powder.

"You're not that stupid, Melissa," Lee Hampton said.

Chapter Six

Melissa was motionless from surprise.

"Why don't you butt out?" the other boy said, his expression threatening.

Lee, still holding Melissa's wrist in a firm grip, met Jack's angry gaze without blinking.

After a moment Jack shrugged. "So, who cares?" he said, and slouched on down the hall.

Left alone with Lee, Melissa looked into his dark, unreadable eyes. "Why?" she demanded. "Why did you do that?"

"Because I—" Then he hesitated, while Melissa's heart took a sudden jump. "Because you deserve better, Melissa," Lee finished, his voice very gentle. He released her arm.

Melissa's heart dropped back into place. "You don't understand," Melissa told him, her voice dull with disappointment. "They—the other kids, everyone—all they see of me is the outside. I feel like I'm wearing a mask. I feel so isolated, so alone."

Some glint of emotion in his face made her pause. She had a swift intuition that Lee Hampton knew what it was like to be alone.

"I'm sorry," she blurted out, wondering what memory she had unwittingly brought forth from his past. "I didn't—"

"It's okay," he told her. "I understand."

He put his arm around her gently, and she laid her cheek against his chest. For the first time in days, Melissa felt alone no longer.

They stood silently together.

Presently Melissa raised her head and stepped back. He made no move to stop her; a belated feeling of embarrassment flooded through her. She couldn't think of what to say. How could he be so understanding and yet so distant?

"How did you get out of class?" Melissa finally said.

"I asked the teacher if I could go check on you."

Melissa was amazed that Lee would admit to interest in her before the whole class. Or had he followed her out of pity? She drew away. Lee did not protest, an omission that was not lost upon Melissa.

"Don't do anything like that again," Lee said.

"I won't." The force of his gaze made her add, "I promise, Lee."

"All right. I guess I'd better get back to class. What are you going to do?"

"Since the whole school has made up its mind that I'm sick," Melissa said bleakly, "I guess I'll check out and go home."

He nodded and walked away without any comment. What a strange guy, Melissa thought. So thoughtful and concerned, and yet so distant. What was he really like?

As she walked down to the office, Melissa examined that question. The answer, however, continued to elude her. After signing the check-out sheet, she turned toward the parking lot, got in her car, and drove off.

When Melissa walked into her home, her mother, still in her robe, was sitting at the kitchen table drinking a cup of coffee. She looked up in surprise when Melissa walked in.

"Melissa! What are you doing home in the middle of the day? Are you all right?" Then she looked again. "You don't mean to say that you wore *that* to school?"

Melissa had been trying hard to shock someone; that it should be her mother was almost funny. But she didn't feel like laughing.

"I was trying to show the kids how ugly I could be." She sat down on the other side of the table.

"Why on earth?"

"It seemed important. It's a little hard to explain." Melissa had remembered a more pressing matter. "Mother, don't we have enough problems?"

Margaret Abbott looked up questioningly.

"I've got a father who's left home. I don't need a wino for a mother!"

Mrs. Abbott laughed. "Melissa, I had two glasses of cooking sherry. Don't you think you're exaggerating just a little?"

"Cooking sherry? That must have tasted dreadful." Melissa, who knew that her father kept wine in the dining room for company dinners, was diverted from her righteous indignation.

"It did. But somehow that seemed to be mine—it came out of the household money, you see. I didn't want any of your father's French wines...silly, I guess." Her mother tried to smile.

"Mother, what's going to happen? And what are all my friends going to think?"

"The thought has occurred to me," her mother said.

"What's going to happen?" Melissa repeated.

"I don't know."

"But I'm scared!"

Margaret Abbott reached over to touch her daughter's hair softly, with a familiar concern that made a lump rise in Melissa's throat. "So am I, sweetheart."

"Oh, Mom." Melissa slipped around the table to hug her mother. "I've been a real jerk, haven't I? Only thinking of myself. I'm sorry."

Her mother answered the hug with a quick squeeze of her own. "I'm sorry, too, about this whole mess. I wish it had never happened."

"So do I." Melissa sat down beside her mother. "Are you really scared?"

Margaret Abbott nodded, her smile a bit forced. "I know you don't think much of my lifestyle, Melissa. But I've spent a lot of time helping your father with his business, even though I wasn't paid. And more recently—well, you think the fashion show is frivolous, and it may be. But we've sold over a hundred tickets already. We're going to raise a lot of money for the children's clinic."

"Oh, Mom." Melissa experienced a wave of remorse. "I'm sorry I said that. I *will* model in the show, if you still want me. I think it's a fine thing to do, and you've done a great job organizing it."

"Thanks," her mother said. "I can use your help. But, even if it's not frivolous, it's not a paying job. I feel very apprehensive about sending out résumés at my age."

"You're not that old," Melissa said.

Her mother's grin was lopsided. "That depends on your point of view. This last week, I've felt pretty ancient."

The worry and apprehension in her eyes were so evident that Melissa dropped her gaze. It didn't seem right. Her mother had always appeared so confident and in control. To see her uncertain frightened Melissa more than she wanted to admit.

"It's all Dad's fault. I hate him!" she said abruptly.

"Don't, Melissa."

"Why not? Aren't you angry?"

"Oh, yes," her mother answered. "Angry, hurt, and—sorry for him."

"Do you still love him?" Melissa whispered, afraid to hear the answer.

Her mother's voice was steady. "I think so," she said. "Love is a hard habit to break."

"Even when people act very badly, like me this week?"

"That wasn't what—"

"I know." Melissa hugged her mother again. Some of the unbearable weight she was carrying seemed to have lifted.

"It helps to talk." Her mother appeared to have read her thoughts. "Do you feel better?"

Melissa nodded.

"I'm glad. What about your day at school? I didn't quite understand about the clothes."

"I wanted to see if the kids at school would like me if I were ugly. I wanted to see what happens when you take away the glamour."

The sadness of her mother's expression was infinite. Melissa bit her lip and wished she hadn't been quite so explicit. "I didn't mean—"

"Of course not."

"Mother," Melissa said, "I'd love you if you looked like the wicked witch of the west!" It was what she herself had yearned for all week, from Tank and Janet and all the other kids, from her absent father.

Her mother laughed. "Tell you what," she said. "Let me get dressed and we'll go out and get a pizza. Okay?"

Later, when Melissa was back in her bedroom, trying without much luck to study for an algebra test, the phone rang.

"Hello?"

"It's me," Janet said awkwardly.

Melissa remembered their quarrel, and, like much that had happened in the last few days, she wished she could erase the whole scene.

"I heard you left school today," Janet said. Then she added, with more candor than tact, "They said you looked awful. Are you sick?"

"Not exactly," Melissa said. "It's sort of complicated."

"Well." Janet still sounded very strange. "I'm not trying to be nosy. I just wanted to ask if you needed your assignments brought home tomorrow."

"Thanks, but I'll probably be back in school." Melissa hesitated, wondering how much genuine concern was behind Janet's offer. The relative distance of the phone conversation lent her courage. "Janet, if I tell you something, will you not say anything at school?"

"Sure."

"My parents have separated. They may get a divorce." The statement was so bald and uncompromising that it made Melissa wince. She waited for some expression of surprise or shock from her friend; instead, there was a long moment of silence.

"It's true, then, what Tonya's been saying," Janet said.

Melissa flushed with anger. "You heard it already? Why didn't you tell me?"

"I didn't think it was true, and I wouldn't repeat that kind of story about my best friend."

There was no doubting the indignation in Janet's voice. Melissa felt a tremor of relief. Maybe Janet really did care.

"Is your mother very upset?"

"She's doing pretty well," Melissa said.

"That's why you've been acting so strangely," Janet commented. "I should have put two and two together. Hang in there, kid."

"Thanks."

"Have you finished that extra-credit assignment for history? It's due tomorrow. If you hand it in late, you won't get the credit."

Melissa groaned. "I forgot all about it. And I've got a test to study for. It's a lost cause, anyway. I failed my last history quiz. I think my grades have sunk beyond redemption."

"Are you kidding? You've been at the top of the class all year. You let that happen!"

"I just can't seem to concentrate these days," Melissa said. "I think my brain has turned to mush!"

"Turned?" Janet teased.

"Okay. Okay. Stop nagging and give me a break, will you?"

There was a silence at the other end of the phone. Melissa knew that she had been needlessly disagreeable, but there was no taking back the words now. After a few more minutes of desultory conversation, the girls hung up. Neither of them felt especially good about their phone call.

Chapter Seven

The next morning when Melissa stopped by Janet's house to pick her up, she discovered that Janet had already left.

"I'm sorry, Melissa. She must have forgotten to call you," Mrs. Donnell said as she tried to pull Jenna's hair into a pigtail. "Be quiet, Jenna, or I'll never get this done before the bus comes! Sorry, Melissa. Janet told us she had to get to school early, so she rode with her dad."

"That's okay, Mrs. Donnell. I'll catch her in class. So long, Mrs. D! See you later, Jenna!"

Melissa made it just in time for the class to begin. She slid into her seat just as Miss Rolo was taking the roll. Janet didn't even look up when she came in. She appeared to be absorbed in her history book.

Miss Rolo launched into the lesson. She was describing the elation of a newly liberated Paris. Her exuberance was contagious. Soon the whole class was joining her rendition of the French national anthem. Melissa forgot her worries as Miss Rolo demonstrated a discreet version of the cancan. The whole class cheered, and Miss Rolo, her plump, pretty face flushed from exertion, executed one last flounce just as Tank Robertson appeared in the doorway.

It was well past the hour, and Melissa waited for Miss Rolo to reprimand Tank. Instead, the teacher merely looked at Tank as the ball player made his way to his desk, his expression stormy. Then, slightly out of breath, she went back to her lesson. The class continued at a more sedate pace until close to the end of the hour.

A quiet knock on the door announced Mr. Cochran, the assistant principal. "Could I borrow you for just a moment, Miss Rolo?"

"Certainly." To the class, the teacher said, "The assignment for tomorrow is to finish reading chapter fourteen." She walked out into the hall and disappeared from view.

There was a general stretching as the class relaxed. Melissa turned her textbook to the proper page and prepared to read. She was too far be-hind—she thought of the uncompleted extra-credit assignment with a sigh—to waste any time. Tank was still sitting at his desk, frowning at the world.

"What's the matter, Tank?" a girl on his other side asked.

Tank snorted. "Old Roly-poly ratted to the coach." His broad hands clenched in anger. "Told him I was about to fail history, and Coach read me the riot act. Darn that woman!"

A boy in the next row laughed. "Better do some work, Robertson."

Tank frowned. "I've got more important things to do than read up on wars that happened before I was born," he complained. "Old Roly-poly is really a pain."

He stood up and began to mimic the teacher's impromptu dance. His clownish movements and broad, heavy frame made the mimicry even more ludicrous.

"'Course I need an extra fifty pounds to play the part." He reached toward the desk in front of him and pulled a heavy cardigan off the back of the seat.

"Hey!" the sweater's owner protested. "Lay off my stuff!"

"Cool it, Liz, it's all for a good cause," Tank said, tying the sweater around his waist. "All I need now is a couple of pillows."

A grinning boy tossed Tank a sweat shirt and Tank stuffed it in his improvised pouch and continued his awkward dancing. "Look at me, the incredible overstuffed Roly-poly, just back from gay Paree!" he sang in a high falsetto, rolling his eyes.

"Cut it out, Tank. You're only making an ass of yourself," Melissa said sharply above the catcalls and laugher of the class.

Then all was silent as the class spotted Miss Rolo with Mr. Cochran right behind her, standing at the threshold. The look on Miss Rolo's face made it quite obvious that she had taken in Tank's performance. Her hurt blue eyes surveyed the class.

"Thank you for your dazzling display of thespian talent, Mr. Robertson," she said, "but right now I suggest you sit down and allow the class to get back to work."

She walked to her desk and sat down without looking at any of her students, who, silent and red-faced, now sat stiffly at their desks.

Mr. Cochran beckoned to Tank. "Young man, you and I have a few things to discuss in my office."

Tank rose from his chair. As he passed in front of Miss Rolo, he cast her a last defiant glance before disappearing down the hall with Mr. Cochran.

The class relaxed. Miss Rolo continued her lesson but the spark had fled. Her usually lively presentation was listless, even slow. Though history was usually one of Melissa's favorite subjects, she was finding the last twenty minutes unbearable. When the bell finally rang, she eagerly pushed through the other students to catch up with Janet.

"What do you think Mr. Cochran will do to Tank?" Janet asked breathlessly by way of a greeting. Her eyes were round with excitement.

"Boiling in oil would be too good for the likes of him!" Melissa said savagely.

"Hey, don't jump down my neck! I had nothing to do with it. I thought it was just as dumb as you did!"

"Sorry. It just makes me so mad!" Melissa said. "And to top it all off, I have to talk to Miss Rolo today about my history report. I forgot to do it after class all because of that stupid Tank."

The bell rang and the two girls dashed off to class.

"Miss Rolo?" Melissa knocked timidly at the teacher's office door.

"Who is it?" Miss Rolo's pleasant voice sounded abstracted.

"It's me, Melissa Abbott. Can I come in and talk to you about that extra history assignment?"

"Of course. Come in. But I haven't graded those papers yet, if that's what you're wondering."

Melissa pushed open the door to find Miss Rolo seated at her desk with several neat piles of students' papers placed on her desk. She looked up and smiled at Melissa. "There's no need to worry. Though it's true that I haven't graded the papers, I did glance at yours, as I've been a little worried about your work lately. I'm happy to say that it looks as though you have gotten over the slump and gone back to your usual outstanding work."

Melissa was dumbfounded. What report? What in heaven's name was Miss Rolo talking about? To her certain knowledge, she had not handed one in. Was Miss Rolo mixing her up with someone else? This was unlikely, as for several years Melissa had been her star pupil. Besides, Melissa had caught a glimpse of her own name on the left-hand top margin of the first paper on one of the piles. It was all too mysterious. It was magic. And who was she to question magic?

"Thank...thank you, Miss Rolo," she managed to stammer before turning to leave. Had she detected an amused twinkle in Miss Rolo's eyes? Was Miss Rolo really her fairy godmother in disguise?

Melissa hurried on down the hall to meet Janet in the parking lot. She could hardly wait to tell her about the mysterious paper.

"Okay," she said, as soon as she reached Janet, waiting by her car. "I just want to know one thing. How did Miss Rolo find a paper with my name on it when I never got to do one?"

Janet's round face turned pink. "I just couldn't stand the thought of your losing your place in the class, Melissa. You needed that credit. I want you to be valedictorian next year."

"But how—"

"You showed me your topic the other day. I did the report last night and put your name on it. I had to get here early to put it on her desk before you came in—"

"Janet, you're a genius! You did a super job— probably better than mine would've been! And I'm a total pig! How could I have said all those mean things to you? I'm really sorry."

"That's okay," Janet said. "There probably was a little bit of truth to them. That's why I got so mad. It is nice to have a friend with pretty clothes she is willing to lend, and to drive around in such a beautiful car. Anyone would enjoy such goodies. But you would be my friend with or without the perks. I want you to know that."

"Thanks," Melissa said, throwing her arms around Janet's neck, causing all their books to scatter to the ground.

As they stooped to pick them up, Janet began to giggle. "Oh, I almost forgot to tell you. Guess what Mr. Cochran made Tank do! Not only did he have to stay after school, which made him late for practice, but the coach made him do laps for getting detention!"

The two girls grinned at each other.

Friday evening seemed long and empty with no date to prepare for. Melissa told herself she didn't care; she hadn't enjoyed her dates with Tank for a long time. Yet the absence of the usual routine left her unsettled and restless.

Finally she took her books up to her room and settled down to study. She owed it to Janet to try to catch up on her schoolwork. After all, she couldn't let her write all her papers for her.

At ten Melissa stretched her cramped muscles and decided to take a break. She wondered if Janet had gotten to go out with Howie, if he had found a car, and whom Tank had gone with, then shook her head at herself.

In the kitchen Melissa peered into the refrigerator and found half an apple pie. Cutting a small piece, she put her plate into the microwave to warm, then sat down at the table with the pie and a glass of milk.

Before she had finished, her mother came into the kitchen. "Get a lot of work done?" she asked.

Melissa nodded.

"Are you okay, sweetheart? Feeling bad about Tank?"

"A little," Melissa told her. "It's not that I miss Tank so much. It just seems strange not to be going out. And I keep wondering what the kids at school will say about it. I can hear them now: 'Poor Melissa, jilted by the team captain.'"

When her mother smiled, Melissa realized the implications of what she had said. If she can smile, Melissa thought, how can I feel glum? All I've lost is a not very worthwhile boyfriend, not a husband of almost twenty years.

She gave her mother a quick kiss on the cheek and put away her dishes before heading back upstairs. She still had that essay to write.

"Don't stay up too late," her mother called after her. "Remember the fashion show is tomorrow."

"Right," Melissa said.

When she sat down at her desk again, she picked up a clean sheet of paper and thought about the topic. Picking up her lit book and skimming the page, a few words caught her eye, and the seemingly dry words suddenly took on new meaning.

After a few moments, Melissa picked up her pen. "'Trust thyself,' Emerson said," Melissa read aloud as she wrote. "A person hates what comes to him by inheritance or gift; such possessions can be taken away; riches can vanish, beauty fade." She could understand that!

"We only possess ourselves—'that which a man is.' If, as Emerson says, nothing can bring you peace but yourself, then first we must find and know ourselves."

By ten past midnight, Melissa had finished a rough draft. Tomorrow she would reread and correct the mistakes and make a clean copy. Then another overdue assignment could be crossed off her list.

The next morning she slept late. When she went downstairs she discovered that her mother, who was in charge of the whole fashion-show production, had already gone. She ate some cereal and hurried to shower and set her hair. She was blowing her hair dry when the phone rang.

It was Janet. "Melissa? Are you coming to pick me up? I told your mother I'd help out backstage."

"Be there in fifteen minutes," Melissa told her friend. "I wish you were modeling, too. I'm getting nervous!"

"You'll be a knockout," Janet reassured her. "You think you're nervous—I have to worry about Jenna!"

Melissa had forgotten that Janet's sister had been recruited as one of the younger models. "Oh, boy," she said, "I think we'll have our hands full."

When they reached the country club, Melissa parked her car and they all hurried into the building.

In the back room set aside for the models, their first impression was of immense disorder. Racks of clothing stood along the sides of the room; a dozen amateur models were pulling on their outfits; anxious faces maneuvered for access to a large mirror.

The girls headed for Melissa's mother, standing beside a rack.

"Thank goodness," she said when she saw them. "You're the last to arrive. We have only half an hour till the show starts."

"What do I do?" Melissa asked.

Her mother handed her a list. "This is a list of your outfits and your number, which gives you your cue. The outfits are on this rack, and your name is on them."

"Good grief," Melissa said, staring at the clothes, and recognizing her mother's handwriting on the papers pinned to each garment. "You really have been working!"

"Yes." Mrs. Abbott rubbed the back of her neck. "Janet, here's Jenna's list. I have her down for only three changes. I didn't want to put the little ones through too much. I'm sure she'll steal the show."

"Let's hope that's all she does," Janet murmured, steering her little sister away from a sequined evening gown. "No, Jenna, that's not yours. Over here."

For the next few minutes Melissa was too busy to be nervous, though she certainly wished she had been at the rehearsal. Then it was her turn for her first walk down the runway in front of the crowded tables. For a moment her self-control wavered, but she forced herself to step out from the wings. After a few steps, she regained her confidence and glided gracefully down the ramp.

Her mother, her voice amplified by the microphone, described the outfit. ". . .jade green complemented by a paisley scarf, the fitted jacket opens to reveal a creamy silk blouse, suit and blouse by Young Miss Fashions."

Melissa slipped off the jacket on cue, turned once more to show the blouse, then headed back for the curtain. She'd hardly had any time to wonder just how many of the women in the audience knew about her parents' separation, how many eyes watched her with pity or speculation.

She had to change quickly. Rushing back toward the racks, she saw Janet, with a firm hold on Jenna. "You looked great," her friend called.

"Thanks," Melissa answered. "How's the mighty mite doing?"

"Cross your fingers," Janet said, then returned her attention to her sister. "Jenna! Don't pull on that button!"

Melissa hurried on. When she made her next trip down the runway, she wore a slacks-and-sweater outfit. This time she almost enjoyed her walk on the ramp. She smiled brightly at the audience. When she came backstage, she saw Janet trying to slip a lace-trimmed nightgown over her little sister's head.

"Hold still, Jenna." Janet sounded impatient.

"Don't want to go to bed!" Jenna insisted.

"You're not going to bed. I just want you to wear the nightgown for a few minutes," Janet explained, firmly pinning down Jenna's arms.

By the time Melissa returned from her next walk, Jenna, looking sulky, was wearing the gown and awaiting her cue.

"Go on, Jenna," Janet whispered. For a moment the little girl resisted, then, obeying a push from her sister, set out down the walkway.

There was a chorus of oh's and ah's from the audience. At first feeling awkward by such obvious approval, Jenna paused midway down the aisle. Then, deciding that this applause was for her, she grinned widely and walked on down to the end. There she stopped, while Mrs. Abbott, smothered laughter in her voice, read her comments on the dainty nightgown.

Janet and Melissa, watching from behind the curtain, shared a relieved grin. "Thank goodness this is her last appearance," Janet whispered. "You never know what Jenna will do next."

They waited expectantly for the little girl to come back up the aisle, but Jenna stood in the middle of the ramp regarding the audience with interest.

"Oh, no," Janet said. "Now what?"

After a moment, the audience began to laugh. Jenna, pleased to be the center of such merriment, stood still and grinned back at them.

"Thank you, Jenna," Mrs. Abbott said over the loudspeaker. "You can go now."

The child didn't move.

"Jenna!" Janet whispered, but the little girl gave her a disdainful glance and turned back to smile at the audience.

"What'll I do?" Janet sounded frantic.

Melissa looked around the cluttered room and saw a box of props in the corner. Hurring over to it, she dug through silk flowers and scarves until she saw a bit of stuffed fur. Pulling it to the surface, Melissa saw that it was an ancient teddy bear. Holding the toy, she hurried back to the entrance.

"Jenna!" Melissa called softly. "Look."

Jenna threw one glance toward them. Her eyes brightened when she saw the animal. "Oh!" she said, holding out her arms.

"No!" Melissa shook her head. "You come here and get it."

Jenna turned and trotted back to the end of the walkway, to laughing applause from the audience. She grabbed the fluffy bear and buried her face in its plush fur, while Janet pulled her quickly out of the way of the next model.

"Never again," Janet murmured, her face still red from vicarious embarrassment.

"Forget it," Melissa told her. "She was the hit of the show."

The rest of the fashion show went smoothly, but the girls were relieved to see it end. The last round of applause was enthusiastic.

"Girls," Melissa's mother said as she came backstage, "you all did a marvelous job. I can't thank you enough. We're going to have a really nice amount to contribute to the children's clinic."

To Melissa and Janet, Mrs. Abbott gave a particularly warm smile, adding to Jenna, who still clung to the teddy bear, "Jenna, you did very well, dear. Thank you for helping us."

The little girl grinned. Janet, still flustered, said, "I'm sorry about—"

"It all worked out very well," Margaret Abbott assured her. To her daughter she said, "Melissa, thank you, too. I appreciate the help when I need it."

Melissa flushed, remembering her earlier refusal. But her mother continued briskly, "Now I've got to get all these clothes packed and back to the right stores.... Oh, I left my notebook out on the podium. Would you run out and get it for me, Melissa?"

"Sure," Melissa said. She made her way past the curtains and down the steps to the main room. A few patrons still lingered, while waiters cleared away the remains of the luncheon. Melissa found the notebook without any problem. Picking it up, she had turned back toward the dressing room when she saw a tall woman, her light brown hair lightly streaked with gray, smiling at her.

Melissa smiled back uncertainly.

"You're Melissa Abbott, aren't you?" the stranger asked. She had a low, pleasing voice.

Melissa nodded.

"I'm Roberta Hampton, Lee's mother. I'd heard him mention your name."

Taken by surprise, Melissa was momentarily silent.

"You are a friend of Lee's?"

"Yes." She tried to sound confident.

Mrs. Hampton brightened visibly. "That's good," she said. "Lee has been rather shy about making friends. I was very glad to hear him speak of you. He needs to get out more with friends his own age."

"He seems a very dedicated student," Melissa said.

Mrs. Hampton nodded. "But even good things can be carried to an extreme, don't you agree?"

Melissa nodded, and was rewarded with another of Mrs. Hampton's warm smiles.

"Come out and see us sometime, Melissa. I'm sure Lee would be glad to see you."

Melissa, who wasn't at all sure, was touched by the obvious sincerity of the invitation. "Thanks," she said. "Maybe I will."

What a surprise—the parents she had pictured as ogres, forcing Lee to work nonstop, expecting nothing less than perfection—how different Mrs. Hampton was from Melissa's speculations! Mrs. Hampton seemed genuinely concerned about Lee.

But, Melissa wondered, if it were not his parents' fault, why did Lee feel so much pressure? There was no immediate answer. She found her mother and delivered the notebook.

"I thought you got lost," her mother said.

"No, I just saw my friend Lee Hampton's mother."

Mrs. Abbott looked up. "Roberta Hampton?" Melissa nodded. "Wonderful people, so giving."

Yeah, Melissa thought. It doesn't make sense.

"Is there anything else I can do to help?"

"I don't think so." Margaret Abbott looked around the room. "I think I've got everything under control."

"I'll take Janet and Jenna home, then," Melissa said. She saw her friend waiting on the other side of the room and made her way over to her.

"Hi." Janet looked rather forlorn.

"What's the matter?"

"That dumb bear." Janet gestured toward the floor, and Melissa saw Jenna sitting cross-legged, still clinging to the stuffed animal. "Jenna won't give him up. I threatened to wallop her bottom, but your mother wouldn't let me. She had to *buy* the old thing so Jenna could take it home."

Melissa laughed. "I'm sure she didn't mind, Janet."

"Oh, she was very nice, said it was only fair in return for Jenna's contribution to the show. Some contribution!" Janet sounded glum. "Bringing the whole production to a standstill."

"It was certainly a memorable performance," Melissa said. "Come on, we'll get ice cream on the way home."

"Ice cream?" Jenna's face brightened. "Can I have chocolate chip?"

"Sure."

Later, when Jenna was safely absorbed in her cone, and dripping only slightly on her dress, Melissa asked, "Did you get to go out with Howie last night?"

"Yes, he borrowed his dad's car. I missed you, Melissa."

"I know." Melissa sighed. "It felt strange to sit home on Friday night."

Janet grinned. "You've been spoiled, honey chile," she drawled. "I've spent plenty of Friday nights at home. Lots of boys will be eager to ask you out, you'll see."

"I don't know." Melissa's voice was thoughtful. "It doesn't always work like that. First, they think I'm Tank's girl, and I don't know how long it will take for that idea to fade. And even then—do you remember our eighth-grade graduation dance?''

"Sure. You were the most beautiful girl there.''

"Maybe.'' Melissa's tone was wry. "But *you* danced all night, and I spent a lot of time sitting at the side of the room, wondering why none of the boys would come close to me.''

"I'd forgotten that.'' Janet looked thoughtful. "Maybe you're so pretty they lose their nerve. Me—I'm such an ordinary—''

"You're cute and funny. Stop putting yourself down,'' Melissa said. "Even with ice cream on your chin.''

Janet grabbed a napkin. "Maybe it's not so easy to be the prettiest girl in school,'' Janet admitted. "I never thought about it like that, Melissa. I thought—I guess everyone thinks—that you've got it made.''

"And they hate me for it,'' Melissa said. "Well, some of them.''

"Just because Tonya is giving you a hard time, don't give up on all the kids at school, Melissa.''

"You're probably right. But I don't like sitting at home.''

"One of the boys will ask you out soon,'' Janet consoled her. "News about you and Tank breaking up will get around. If necessary, I'll carry a sign through the halls!''

"Don't you dare—"

Janet grinned. "Oh, all right. But what about the spring dance? Has Tank broken that date, too?"

"I'm not really sure," Melissa admitted.

"Well." Janet sounded horrified. "You *have* to go to the spring formal. Good grief, what if they elect you May Queen and you're not there! You can't do that!"

"Janet, brace yourself. Now don't faint from shock," Melissa said. "But I don't think I want to be May Queen."

"But, Melissa!" Janet looked astonished. "The May Queen is the prettiest girl in school!"

"That's why," Melissa said.

Janet stared at her. "Hey, you're just feeling down. You'll get over this. Some nice guy will ask you out, I'm sure of it."

"There's nobody I want to go out with," Melissa said. Unbidden, Lee's dark eyes and rare smile surfaced in her mind's eye. "Nobody at all."

Chapter Eight

Sunday morning Melissa went to church with her mother, but she didn't stay for Sunday school.

"Aren't you going to the picnic?" Mrs. Abbott asked as they walked toward the car.

Melissa shook her head. Her mother frowned but didn't comment.

At home, Melissa changed into jeans, and they ate a light lunch. Stacking the dishes, her mother said, "I promised Cousin Louise I'd come out for a little while this afternoon. Would you like to come?"

"No, thanks," Melissa told her. "I think I'm

going over to Lee Hampton's house. I need to ask him a question about algebra.''

She had, after all, been invited, Melissa told herself. The problem was, it was Lee's mother who had issued the invitation. What would Lee think if she turned up on his doorstep?

Would he show her the understanding she had glimpsed so briefly, or withdraw behind the wall of reserve that was his usual sanctuary? If she thought about going for too long, she would lose her nerve.

Melissa checked the address in the school directory, grabbed her car keys, and went.

She found the Hampton residence without any problem; it was brick, two story, set on a large, carefully maintained lot with large oak trees shading the house. The driveway was wide; in front of the garage two cars sat gleaming amid puddles of water.

"He really did wash the cars," Melissa said to herself. It hadn't just been a dumb excuse, then. But still, if he'd wanted to go with her, there were other times for car washing.

Melissa parked her car, wondering if she should have come. The temptation to leave was strong, but she forced herself to get out of her car.

The front entrance to the house was imposing; Melissa turned toward the back. Maybe she could get a glimpse of Lee outdoors. Instead, as she rounded the corner of the house, Melissa found Mrs. Hampton pulling weeds from a row of shrubs along the patio.

"Why, hello, Melissa. How nice to see you."

"I—I thought I'd drop by for a few minutes. Is—is Lee home?" Melissa felt foolish.

Mrs. Hampton didn't seem to feel that her unannounced visit was anything out of the ordinary. "He's downstairs in the rec room. Come in and I'll show you the way."

She led Melissa through the French doors, past a sunny dining room and into the kitchen. "Would you like a soft drink?"

"No, thanks."

Mrs. Hampton turned just as the phone on the wall rang. Pausing, she lifted the receiver.

"Why, hello, Jennifer. Just a second." Mrs. Hampton motioned toward the door on the far wall. "Go on down, Melissa. It's just at the bottom of the stairs."

"Thanks," Melissa told her. She walked slowly down the narrow stairway, her heart suddenly pounding and her mouth dry. What would she say to Lee?

When she reached the wide basement room at the bottom, the light from the shallow windows was dim, and she paused to allow her eyes to adjust. A sudden movement made her jump.

The figure in the middle of the room whirled in mock attack. Melissa gasped, but the sound was lost in the snap of a hard kick. It was Lee, dressed in loose-fitting black pants and a jacket tied with a dark belt. It was a costume familiar from martial-arts films, but Melissa had never before seen anyone practice the lethal kicks and punches. She watched silently, with interest.

She was so still in the shadow at the foot of the stairs, and Lee was so absorbed in his practice that he didn't appear to notice her arrival.

She felt renewed admiration for this quiet, studious boy as she glimpsed a side of him that she had never dreamed of. There was a sinewy strength to his slender frame that she had not realized before, and the controlled grace of his motions was thrilling to watch.

With one final kick and a slashing movement of his arm, Lee came to a halt. For the first time he looked toward her. His face—so intent during his practice—went blank with surprise.

Melissa, afraid to speculate about what he might be feeling, spoke softly. "Hi."

"Hello, Melissa," Lee answered. His voice was low and as controlled as usual; he seemed hardly out of breath.

"You're very good," Melissa told him. "I didn't know you were interested in the martial arts.... What kind—I mean—"

"Tae Kwon Do," he said.

Melissa looked more closely at his costume. "Is that—are you—"

"A black belt. Yes." Melissa caught the faintest hint of pride. "I've been studying since I was ten years old."

"That's incredible, Lee," Melissa said. "You're a fascinating person, do you know that? Why do you keep so much to yourself? Don't you want to have friends?"

He looked away from her puzzled gaze. "I don't fit in, you know that. And I don't have time to waste."

"I know." Melissa's tone hardened despite her best intentions. "You have to keep your four-oh average. Don't you have time for *people?*"

"I do all right on my own. Maybe I'm just a private person."

Melissa felt as if the chill of the basement room had seeped down inside her. "I'm sorry," she said. "You mother said to come down. I didn't mean to interrupt."

In a corner of her mind she heard Janet's words: *Any boy at school would jump at the chance to go out with you.* If Janet only knew!

Lee seemed to have followed the direction of her thoughts. "That's not what I—" He seemed embarrassed, too. "Everyone at school likes you, Melissa. Why would you, I mean—"

"I don't want to be liked for my looks or my tennis serve or my cheerleading," Melissa told him. "I thought you understood that. I thought—I don't know why—that you might like me just for being me. I'm sorry I barged in."

She ran up the steps before Lee could sense the tears she held back. What a fool she had been! What had ever given her the idea that she and Lee could be friends!

She slipped quietly out of the house without even saying good-bye to Mrs. Hampton.

"Did you have fun with Howie Friday?" Melissa asked Janet as they walked through the halls to history class on Monday.

"You bet! We went bowling. It's such a joy not to have to do the same thing every weekend. Tank's a real movie nut, isn't he?"

"Unfortunately. And always the worst movies, too." Melissa was secretly wondering whom Tank had escorted to the movies on Friday. Janet answered her unspoken question.

"Carol Whittard."

"Who's she?"

"The new girl from Atlanta. The cute redhead."

"Oh. Do we have any classes with her? I can't seem to place her—"

Janet assumed a lofty air. "She's a senior, my dear. An older woman."

"Oh, la-dee-dah!" Melissa giggled.

"Glad you think it's a joke, but what about the spring formal? Are you still going with Tank?"

"I'm not sure," answered Melissa. "We haven't exactly talked about it."

"I can't believe he would dump you the week before the dance! Even Tank wouldn't sink that low!"

"That's what I intend to find out," Melissa said grimly.

All through her history class, Melissa was trying to decide what she would say to her ex-boyfriend about the spring prom. The class dragged on interminably. Ever since Tank's impersonation, Miss Rolo had toned down her presentation. She was no longer given to the flights of fancy that had so enlivened her earlier classes. Now her students stirred restlessly, occasionally exchanging furtive notes. Only Tank looked placidly cheerful. *Typical,* thought Melissa disgustedly. Nevertheless, she was determined to accost him as soon as the bell sounded.

When it finally did, she jumped up and ran after him.

"Tank—" she said.

Tank turned. "Oh, hi, Melissa," he said awkwardly. "How you doing?"

Several students paused to stare curiously, but Melissa plunged on. This was definitely not the moment for small talk, especially as Tank's eyes were roaming the hall and he was checking his watch as though he didn't know already that the tardy bell would ring any moment.

"Tank," Melissa said desperately, "are we going together to the dance Friday night?"

Tank checked his watch again. "Well," he said, "as captain of the football team, I guess I have a duty—"

"What?"

"I mean, it's sort of a tradition, you know, to escort the May Queen—" he stammered.

Duty? Tradition? Melissa was so angry she could barely speak. She could feel her face getting hot as she struggled for control. "Tank," she said, "I don't think you get the picture. For one, the students haven't even voted yet. I may not even be Queen. Besides, I don't want to be Queen. So put that idea out of your head. If you go with me, you won't be going with the Queen, but with me, Melissa Abbott."

"Huh?" He looked genuinely puzzled. "Everyone knows you're going to get it. What're you worried about?"

"I'm not worried. I've just decided I'm not interested in that sort of thing anymore—"

"That's dumb," Tank interrupted. "Who wouldn't want to be named the prettiest girl in school?"

"Me," Melissa said. "I am not going to be May Queen, Tank. That's a promise. If they elect me, I'll decline."

Tank flushed. "If that's your idea of of a joke—"

"It's no joke."

"If that's the way you feel"—Tank's voice rose—"I've got my reputation to think about, you know."

"Fine," Melissa said. "Then we'll just call the whole thing off."

She told Janet at lunch. "It's official. I'm not going to the spring dance with Tank. His reputation wouldn't survive it."

"What are you talking about?" Janet asked.

"It's too complicated," Melissa said, poking a French fry into a dab of ketchup. "But the date's off."

"That's the lowest thing I ever heard! A week—not even a week—before the dance! Just who does he think he is? You've already got a new formal."

Melissa thought of the pale blue gown that she and her mother had picked out a month ago, and that now hung swathed in plastic in the back of her closet. "There'll be other dances," she said.

"I wonder who Tank will ask," Janet said. "Most of the girls already have dates, too. I'd love to see *him* without a date."

"He'll come up with someone," Melissa predicted.

"Tank asked the new girl, Carol, to the dance. He told Howie at practice," Janet informed Melissa during the course of their nightly phone call.

"I guess he's set, then," Melissa said.

"No! She turned him down. She has a boyfriend in college who's coming up to take her. Isn't it rich?"

"Wonderful," Melissa agreed.

Their satisfaction was short-lived. When Melissa and Janet went to the gym Friday afternoon to help hang decorations for the big dance, the first person they encountered was Tonya Phillips, surrounded by a group of girls all listening intently to Tonya's high-pitched chatter.

A couple of the girls looked at Melissa nervously, but Tonya raised her voice. "And then he said, 'Would you like to go to the dance with me?' I guess he thinks that Melissa isn't going to win. Nobody wants to be stuck with a loser!"

Melissa decided that she would meet this one head on. "Are you going to the dance with Tank, Tonya? I'm really glad. I hope you guys have a great time."

Tonya looked startled. "W-well. . .yes, as a matter of fact, he did ask me. . .and, uh. . .I said yes."

Melissa smiled. "See you later."

She and Janet walked toward the group hanging streamers.

"Well, that settles that," said Janet. "You were really great! Did you notice that Tonya actually had the grace to blush?"

"Sure did! Well, wait till those Friday dates. I bet she'll just love those old horror movies—not to mention Tank's ideas of making out."

Janet giggled. "Maybe she'll go for that. They're well suited—"

"I agree—two peas in a pod."

"But how does Tank feel about not taking the May Queen?"

"Janet, I hate to tell you, but I'm not going to be the beauty queen."

"What are you talking about? You're the prettiest girl in the school. Everyone agrees!"

"Well, I went to Mr. Cochran this morning and asked him to take my name off the ballot."

"Are you out of your gourd? How could you have done such a thing?"

Melissa confessed, "That's more or less what Mr. Cochran said—"

"Well, I totally agree with him! How did you explain it?"

"I told him that being pretty just isn't enough."

"And he took that?"

"Well, he didn't argue anymore."

There was a pause. Then Janet said, "Well, Melissa, it's your life, but frankly, I don't understand. Being pretty doesn't sound so bad to me. I hope you don't regret your decision when everyone else has gone to the prom—"

"I won't," Melissa promised. She moved over to the window and helped a petite brunette with a crimson streamer she was trying to drape.

"Are you going to the big event, Kathy?" she asked, quite sure of an affirmative response.

Kathy colored and shook her head.

Perhaps for the first time Melissa realized that there were many girls who had not had her opportunities.

"I didn't go last year, either," Kathy volunteered. Her voice was wistful.

"That's okay. I'm not going, either," Melissa said. "Hey, watch that bow there! It's supposed to be more in the middle." Melissa Abbott, she told herself, you really are a spoiled brat! She concentrated on the decorating and asked no more questions.

Chapter Nine

The decorating crew finished the gym by five. Then Melissa and Janet drove home.

"Melissa," Janet said, "are you sure you wouldn't like to go with Howie and me? There'd be plenty of boys dying to dance with you."

"And plenty of dates ready to stab me in the back!" Melissa's tone was dry. "No, thanks. Besides, after breaking a date with Tank, that wouldn't be exactly *'comme il faut,'* as my mother would say."

"What?"

"Not the thing to do."

"Oh."

When they reached Janet's house, Janet collected her books and got out of the car. "What will you do tonight?" she asked.

Melissa shrugged. "Read a good book?" Yet, in spite of herself, she had a few lingering doubts. Had she done the right thing? The whole school would be bewildered at her stepping aside. But, then, it wasn't the school's decision.

After parking her car in her garage, Melissa let herself into the house. A note on the refrigerator said:

Be back before you leave. I put your dress out.

Mother

Good grief! Melissa thought. She hadn't yet had the nerve to tell her mother that she wasn't going to the dance. She climbed the stairs and saw the new formal laid out across her bed. It was a lovely dress, ice blue with small capped sleeves and a curving neckline.

She didn't want to look at the dress. Putting her books on her desk, Melissa went downstairs and made herself a sandwich. But she was too restless to eat. She went downstairs to the den and flipped on the television.

Ten minutes later, Melissa realized that she didn't even know what she was watching. She shut off the TV and went back upstairs.

She had to get out of the house. Reaching for the notepad on the counter, Melissa scribbled a hasty note:

Gone to library, back at ten. Explain later.
Melissa

She put the small slip of paper under a magnet on the front of the refrigerator and went to the closet for her jacket.

On a Friday night, the branch library was almost deserted. Melissa picked up a couple of magazines and headed for the back of the building.

Flipping open a magazine, she tried to concentrate on the page, but the words couldn't hold her attention. She thought of the streamers they had hung in the gym, the lights that would shine tonight, making the usually prosaic room look a little different, special. What would the kids think when she didn't show up?

Or would they even notice? One of the other girls in the court would be crowned May Queen, and life at Forest Hill High would go on as usual.

Maybe she had made her grand gesture for nothing.

But it had been right for her; Melissa was still sure. No one else might understand, but to stand there tonight in a pretty dress and hear the applause of the crowd would be more than she could stand.

Looking idly through the pages at an elegantly decorated house, she thought of her mother. She had a real eye for color, a talent for design. She should have studied, found more of an outlet for her talents rather than coordinating fashion shows for charity. Was that what came of too much beauty and charm? Did it turn you away from developing talents and stifle ambition? Not if Melissa had anything to say about it.

She was in a kind of sleepy daydream when a frowning face suddenly loomed over her. "Lee!" Melissa exclaimed.

"What are you doing here?" he demanded angrily.

"It's—why shouldn't I be here?"

"When most of the school is expecting..."— he glanced at his watch—"...was expecting you at the spring formal? Your mother is frantic because she doesn't know where you are."

"I left a note."

"She didn't find it," Lee told her. His tone was still stern. "She called my house to see if you could be there. She sounded upset."

"But I don't understand. I did leave a note, Lee."

"Such erratic behavior isn't like you, she said." Lee ignored her protest.

"What's erratic about sitting quietly in a library?" she demanded, her voice rising. Several people turned to stare at them.

"The night of the biggest dance of the whole year?" Lee asked incredulously. Melissa winced. Did Lee see her as no more than a social butterfly?

"But that's why, Lee—that's the whole thing!" She stood up to confront him and saw that more people were watching them curiously.

"We can't talk here," she said, lowering her voice. "Let's go outside."

He followed her without a word. When they reached the parking lot, she turned to look at him. In the shadows his face looked stern and unapproachable.

How could she make him understand? She wasn't even sure she understood herself.

"Come on," Lee told her. "We'll go get a Coke. I want to hear what you have to say."

"I don't think it really matters," Melissa began. "Besides, my car—"

"I'll bring you back to get it later. I don't want you out of my sight."

Rather than argue, Melissa climbed obediently into the brown station wagon and sat primly on the far side while Lee backed the car out of its parking space.

The drive to a fast-food restaurant was a silent one. But when they pulled in under the glaring neon sign, Lee said, his voice calmer, "I think you'd better call your mother."

Melissa nodded. Digging out a coin from her purse, she went to the pay phone at the side of the lot, while Lee stood in line to buy some soft drinks. She dialed her home number once, then again, but could get only a busy signal. I'll have to try later, she thought. When she went back to the car, Lee had returned. She climbed back in the car and he handed her a tall paper cup full of ice and bubbling soda.

"Now, would you mind telling me why you didn't go to the dance?" he demanded.

"I didn't have a date."

"What happened to Tank?"

"I—we broke the date."

"Why?"

"I told him I wasn't going to be May Queen. He seemed to think that I would have been the one chosen."

"The whole school was expecting you to be Queen," Lee said. "Why did you turn it down?"

"Because I'm trying to find out who Melissa Abbott is—behind the makeup and the clothes. The outside keeps getting in the way. I want to know who *I* am, Lee, and I want to know who cares about me just for being me, not just for the titles that I can win."

She had lost the calm thread of her beginning and her voice threatened to break. Lee seemed far away, and she could not read in his dark eyes what he was thinking.

She had gripped her hands together tightly in her lap. He put out one hand to touch hers; his fingers, even in the dim light, were dark against her own pale skin, but she could feel their comforting strength. She turned toward him and saw that the dark enigmatic eyes smiled at her.

"Beauty on the outside doesn't preclude beauty on the inside," he told her.

Melissa swallowed hard. "That's the nicest thing anyone has ever said to me," she choked out.

He raised his hand to touch her cheek.

"You're a pretty girl," Lee said. "You can't expect other people not to respond to your looks. But you can show them that you're more than a pretty face. You can do that, Melissa." His face was very close to hers. Was he going to kiss her?

Beyond their car, an older woman in a blue sedan watched them, disapproval showing clearly on her face. Melissa blushed. Lee, following her gaze, grinned and took his hand away from her cheek.

"I'd better take you home," he said.

Melissa nodded, remembering the aborted phone call. Yet she didn't want to say good-night yet. She wanted to prolong the closeness that she felt with Lee. She was disappointed by his swift change to a matter-of-fact attitude.

"Are you going to be all right?" he asked as she got out of the station wagon.

"Oh, sure." Melissa's tone was flat. She slammed the door of her little compact and started the engine. Afterward she thought that it was her own frustration that made her jerk the wheel too far as she made the turn out of the lot. She felt the car lurch and heard the impact, too late.

Lee, behind her, was already out of his car.

"What'd I hit?"

"The curb," Lee said. "Which wouldn't have mattered, except that the concrete is broken and it's made a big gash in your tire."

"Great."

"Back your car into the lot and out of the driveway. You're not going anywhere like that."

When she had pulled the car back into a parking space, Melissa got out to look at her damaged tire, now flat as a pancake.

"I don't think it can be patched. We'd better go look for another tire. Do you know the size?" Lee asked.

Melissa shook her head. Lee knelt to get a closer look at the tire in the dim light of the streetlamp, then stood again. "Come on, we'll go check some gas stations."

In the next two hours Melissa learned more about tires than she wanted to know. She discovered that her small foreign car was not the easiest automobile to find parts for. One gas station attendant after another shook his head; the last one directed them to a garage, but it had closed.

Lee finally shrugged in defeat. "I think we'll have to wait until tomorrow. Your car should be all right at the parking lot. I'll take you home."

When they were a few blocks away from Melissa's house, Melissa couldn't resist asking, "Why don't you like me, Lee?"

Surprised, he turned to look at her and slowed the car. "I do like you, Melissa. You know that."

"No," she said. "I don't. The only time you talk to me is when I'm in trouble. The rest of the time you ignore me. What's wrong with me, Lee?"

Lee pulled over to the side of the quiet residential street and stopped the car.

"Of course I like you. Everybody at school—well, almost everybody," he amended at her grimace, "likes you."

"Then why don't you ever talk to me at school, sit with me at lunch, even..."—Melissa felt her face flush, but she persisted—"...ask me out?"

The silence was almost painful. "I guess I thought that you were busy with other people, Melissa. I never really imagined that you'd be interested in someone like me."

"Why not?" Melissa demanded. "Why shouldn't I like you?"

"I'm not a popular sort of—"

"If I ever hear that word again, I'm going to scream," Melissa said fiercely.

Lee grinned. "Okay. But you could have any boy in school as your friend, Melissa. I don't know why you picked me. I can't play tennis. I don't know how to dance."

"You could learn if you wanted to," Melissa said. "If you don't want to, who cares?"

"I guess I've been too busy to make any friends," Lee said. "I have to—"

"I know." Melissa's tone was angry. "Your grades! Don't you think you're a little fanatical about your schoolwork?"

Silence again. Melissa was aware of Lee, the shadows that hid his face, and how far away he seemed in the darkness.

"Melissa," he said slowly, "I'm not like everyone else.... I was adopted when I was six."

"That doesn't matter—" Melissa began.

But Lee didn't allow her to finish. "It matters to me." His voice was urgent. "I was too old, Melissa. I remember too much."

There was so much anguish in his voice that Melissa bit back her response.

"I don't remember my parents, not really. I remember someone holding me, a soft voice. But I remember the bombs, and people screaming. I had nightmares for years, Melissa. I'd wake up yelling, trying to escape walls of fire. I was in a refugee camp in Laos when Dr. Hampton found me. He'd been on a fact-finding mission, and he stayed three months when he saw the children who were dying for lack of care. I was ill, along with hundreds of others.... I always wondered what made him choose me."

Melissa swallowed. Now she understood. Vietnam. Her experiences were so trivial compared to Lee's! How could she have made such a big deal about them? "But it's over now," she cried. "The war's over now! You're safe! You have a family who loves you."

"But what about the children who didn't escape, Melissa?" Lee queried. "Why did I live when so many died?"

"You feel guilty," Melissa said. It was a revelation to her. "Lee, you're working yourself to death, driving yourself like this because you feel guilty that you were saved? There's no reason—"

"I owe them something," he said painfully. "I *have* to do well, Melissa, or nothing makes any sense. I owe it to the Hamptons, and to the children that lay in the cots beside me and didn't make it...."

Melissa reached across the darkness that lay between them and found his hand. Holding it tightly, she tried to make him listen. "Lee, you can't spend the rest of your life trying to make up for the past, for wrongs that were beyond your control. You don't have to feel guilty because you survived. You can't play God...and the Hamptons—they wanted a child to love, Lee. You don't have to repay anything, prove yourself worthy... Your mother—" Melissa faltered. Then she continued in a firmer tone: "Your *mother's* worried about you, Lee. She knows you're pushing yourself too hard, and she's concerned that you don't have friends. Everyone needs friends, Lee. I'd like to be your friend."

Melissa let go of his hand to look at Lee, but she couldn't see his expression in the darkness. Then she felt his arm slide around her shoulders to pull her closer. Instinctively, she lifted her face for their first kiss.

His lips were firm and warm when they found hers.

She could hear his breath coming quickly, and she felt her own heart thump against his chest.

When they drew apart he said, reaching for the ignition key, "I think I'd better get you home."

Even in the dark she could see his hand was shaking. Her heart was still beating so fast and so hard she was sure that he could hear it.

He started the car, tucking Melissa's hand in the crook of his arm as he drove. She dropped her head on his shoulder.

When they reached her driveway, she asked shyly, "Would you like to come in and watch TV for a while?"

"If it's all right with your mother."

Melissa suddenly remembered the incompleted phone call. "Horrors! I've got to explain!"

"Relax," Lee said. "She's probably found the note by now, anyway."

Melissa slipped the key into the front door and turned the handle to open it. As she entered, she bumped into a tall masculine presence.

"Dad!" she exclaimed in astonishment. "What in the world are you doing here?"

"I could well ask the same question of you, young lady," Mr. Abbott said, his voice thickened by fury.

One look at his flushed face was enough to drive away thoughts of Melissa's anticipated pleasant evening. "I—I went to the library," she stammered. "I left Mother a note on the refrigerator—"

Her mother, dressed in a robe, hurried up and laid a restraining hand on her husband's arm. "Just a minute, Ron. Let the child explain!" She turned a puzzled face to Melissa. "Melissa? The library? What about the dance? Where's Tank?"

"Sneaking around with some boy we don't even know!" Her father shouted. "I went to the school tonight expecting to see my beautiful daughter as the May Queen and she wasn't even there. You surely don't expect us to believe—"

The torrent of his words unlocked in Melissa all the negative emotions she had felt all week. "You have the nerve to question me," she asked, her voice trembling, "after all that you've done to Mom and me? You were disappointed not to see me as the beauty queen just to flatter your own ego! Looks are all that matter to you— looking good! You don't care about the person behind the looks at all! If you're so stuck on looks, why didn't you enter your secretary in the contest? She's just about the right age—''

The ugly words hung in the air between them, and they could not be recalled.

Ron Abbott looked as if he'd been hit. His face had paled. Melissa turned away blindly and collided with Lee, still steady and calm, who reached out for her.

"Lee," she whispered, "I'm sorry."

"It's okay," he murmured.

He held her for a moment and his firmness steadied her. "I think I'd better go," he told her. "I'll call you tomorrow. Good night, Mr. and Mrs. Abbott." He closed the door quietly behind him.

Melissa's father ran his hand over his face. "Melissa," he began, "I didn't mean...we do trust you, you know that. But we didn't know where you were."

"I did leave a note!" Melissa spoke mainly to her mother, regretting the lines of worry she saw, the weariness in her mother's face. "It was on the refrigerator. I meant to tell you earlier about the dance, but I was afraid you might not understand. I broke the date with Tank. I didn't want the crown.... I'm sorry if you were worried."

"It's all right now, " Mrs. Abbott said. "You're home safe and sound." She smiled shakily at Melissa.

"I should have told you before," Melissa said.

"Was that Lee?" her mother asked. "He seems like a nice boy. I'm sorry he had to witness a family upset. Next time we'll meet him properly."

Melissa looked from her mother to her dad. The scene had left them all drained. "Good night, Mother, good night, Dad," she said. "I'm going to bed. I'll explain everything in the morning." She didn't look back at the two motionless figures standing side by side in the hall.

Chapter Ten

Wow! What a weekend!'' Janet's tone was one of awe. ''What happened Saturday?'' Janet asked as she and Melissa drove toward school.

''Lee drove me to the garage so I could buy a tire for my car,'' Melissa told her. ''Then we went to his house and his mother made us lunch. She seemed really pleased to see me. We spent the afternoon in the rec room playing pool.''

''Is that all?'' Janet said teasingly.

''Well''—Melissa grinned—''just about.''

''Are your parents still mad?''

''Mom's not,'' Melissa said. ''She found my note under the refrigerator. I must have knocked it off the door. And she likes Lee. She agrees he's an improvement over Tank. I think she understands about the dance."

"It's a shame you didn't get to wear your new dress," Janet said.

"There'll be other dances." Melissa's tone was untroubled.

"That's a relief. I was afraid you'd sworn off dances for life!"

As Melissa parked the car in the school lot, Janet asked, "Are you ready for your speech?"

Melissa's mind went blank. "What speech?"

"Melissa Abbott! The student council elections—you know! You make your speech this morning. Don't tell me you're going to pull out of that, too, not after I've been making posters for a week!"

Melissa looked guilty.

"Enough is enough, Melissa!" Janet was indignant. "If you drop out, that only leaves John Barton for president. Remember John? When we worked hours setting the field up for the Cancer Jogathon, he's the guy who was in the corner flirting with the girls. You can't wish him on the students. Give them a choice, for Pete's sake."

"Okay," Melissa said reluctantly. "I'll say something."

"Good," Janet said. "Now hurry, we'll be late for history."

"Late? It's ten minutes before the first bell."

"Don't you know what day it is?"

Melissa shook her head.

"It's Miss Rolo's birthday."

"Is it?" Melissa asked. "We should have done something."

"*Should?* Melissa Abbott, you've had your head so full of your own problems, you don't even know what's happening around you. Come on."

When they took their seats, Melissa saw that almost all the class had assembled early. Tank was missing, but most of the seats were filled. A huge cake, complete with lighted candles, was sitting on Miss Rolo's desk.

"Ready?" Janet asked. "Here she comes."

The class broke into a raucous rendition of "Happy Birthday" as Miss Rolo walked in the door.

"Oh, my," Miss Rolo said, for once at a loss for words. "Well!"

"Read the card," Janet told her.

Miss Rolo opened the card slowly. "To a terrific teacher and a beautiful person," she read. "Best wishes from your first-period class."

"Thank you," she said, smiling broadly. Then, with a wink, she added, "If you think this is a bribe to shorten the final exam—"

Everyone laughed. "That's great," Melissa whispered to Janet beneath the general conversation. "I wish I'd thought of it."

Janet's grin was a bit rueful. "You were the only one who had the guts to tell Tank what you thought of his trick. After that, we felt we had to do something, too."

Melissa was sitting in a row with the other candidates, looking out over the packed auditorium, at the student council meeting. When her turn came, she walked to the microphone and spoke with confidence.

"I came here this morning thinking of withdrawing," she told them. "But someone told me that the students deserve a choice, and that's true. Most of you know that I've served on the student council for three years. I've worked at almost every event we've sponsored. I've decorated and cleaned up after dances, organized bake sales and washed cars. I planned for the Special Olympics last fall and organized the student art show at Christmas.... I've done my best for you. If you choose to elect me, I will do my best again. All I ask is that you vote for the person you think will make the best president—not for the prettiest, or the most popular. Vote for the best qualified. The choice is yours. I will trust your judgment."

The audience applauded enthusiastically. Janet grinned at her from the side, and farther back Melissa exchanged a glance with Lee.

Melissa was late getting out of the auditorium. She had to wait for all the other students to leave, and then hear some boring speech from the principal. When she finally got to leave, she was late for lunch.

Melissa paused in the entrance to the cafeteria, looking around for Janet. Tank came up and threw an arm casually around her.

"Great speech, doll," he said. "This time next week I'll be taking out the new president."

She tried to step away. "You must be joking."

"About the speech?"

"No, about us," Melissa said. "After all that's happened, you don't really think that I want to go out with you?"

"Hey," Tank told her. "We've been going together since last fall. Everyone has fights. What's the big deal? You and me, we're leaders. We just sort of naturally belong together."

"Tank, you really are dense," Melissa said. "Let go of me, please."

Tank's hold on her tightened. "Nobody puts me down like—" he began.

Melissa looked up to see Lee Hampton watching them.

"Take your hands off my girl, Robertson," Lee told him. "You heard the lady."

"Listen, you pipsqueak, you don't tell me what to do." Tank's tone was outraged. But he let go of Melissa. She stepped backward, almost colliding with Janet. Several other students had gathered to stare.

"Melissa!" Janet hissed. "Stop him! He'll murder Lee!"

"I doubt it," she said smugly.

"Lay off, Robertson," Lee said.

"Listen, this is between me and my girl," Tank said menacingly, stepping forward.

"I'm not—" Melissa began, but she paused as Tank reached out to shove Lee away. Before anyone could see what had happened, he lay sprawling face down on the floor. Lee, looking untouched, stood over him.

"What happened?" Janet gasped.

"I think Tank's reputation was just shattered," Melissa said. "Let's go, Lee."

The votes were cast after lunch. Melissa, going out to tennis practice, tried not to think about anything but getting her serve in the right place. She was alone on the end court when a familiar figure walked past the fence.

"Hello, Tonya," Melissa called.

The other girl stopped. Her face wore its usual expression of discontent.

"You tried out for the tennis team last year, didn't you?" Melissa asked.

Tonya nodded. "I didn't make it. I got cut the first round."

"I remember," Melissa told her. "You were pretty bad."

Tonya stiffened. "So I can't afford private lessons, like *some* people!"

"There are other ways to learn." Melissa's tone was even. "Coach Allan is always willing to help the kids. Why don't you ask him for some pointers? Come out and practice after school. Let him see you working, see if you can improve. Then try out again for the team next year and see what happens."

"Why should I?"

"Nobody's forcing you," Melissa said. "But you can't keep blaming me and hating me because of what I have. I'm really sick of it. You make me miserable, and yourself, too. Do something for yourself, instead of just complaining all the time."

Tonya flushed. "Are you making fun of me?"

"No," Melissa said. "I'm trying to give you some good advice."

Tonya was silent for a moment. Then she said, "I can't practice alone."

"I'll work out with you a couple of times a week, if you start working on your serve and do your board work," Melissa told her.

"Why would you want to help me?"

"Why not? I think you'd be a good player. All you need is a few lessons."

Tonya was surprised into a friendly smile. "Okay," she said. "I'll think about it."

"You do that." Melissa hit her last ball, then went to collect the balls on the other side of the net.

Janet met her as she headed for the parking lot. "I thought you'd gone home," Melissa said.

"No," Janet said. "I waited till the teachers finished counting the ballots. Congratulations, Madam President!"

Melissa hesitated. "I hope they voted for me for the right reasons," she said.

Janet groaned. "Melissa Abbott! You can't spend the rest of your life trying to second-guess the world. Enough!"

"Okay." Melissa grinned. "I'm happy, okay?" But inside her, a small sense of doubt lingered. Would she have to face that doubt for the rest of her life? But the problem no longer seemed more than she could handle. She would know herself, and from that knowledge would come the grace to accept both her triumphs and her defeats.

"Hurry up," she told Janet.

"What's the rush?"

"Lee's coming over to study with me," Melissa told her.

"Sounds like fun." Janet winked.

When Melissa got home she threw her books on the foyer table. "Hi, Mom! I'm home!"

"I'm in my room!" her mother called back.

Melissa rushed up the steps and paused at her mother's door. "Wow! You look really nice."

"Thanks. I'm going out for dinner tonight. I left some cold cuts in the refrigerator. I hope you don't mind eating alone."

"No, that's fine. Lee and I are going out for a snack anyhow. Then we're going to work on algebra at his house." Melissa walked into the bedroom and sat down on the bed. "So, who are you going out with? Katie?"

Her mother continued applying her makeup. "No, your father."

"Dad?" Melissa repeated. "Are you guys getting back together?"

"We just want to talk about it," her mother told her. "It's only a possibility, Melissa. Nothing definite, either way."

Melissa stared at her. A little while ago she would have done anything to get her parents back together. Now she wasn't sure how she felt.

Mrs. Abbott saw her daughter's confused expression in her reflection in the mirror and she turned to her daughter and sat down on the bed next to her. "Oh, Melissa, it's so hard to explain. I'm not blind to what's been going on, and I know you're not, either. It's just that, well, when you've been married to someone for so long, when you've worked hard with a person and raised a child, it's hard just to throw it all away." She put her arms around Melissa, and they hugged for a few lingering moments. "I don't know if I can forgive him, but I'm going to try. And if I can, I hope you can, too." Her mother pulled away and smiled into her daughter's eyes. "You know, these past weeks have taught me something. We are both really a lot stronger than I thought. Whatever comes of this, Melissa, whether your father and I work it out or not, I'll survive. And so will you." She stood up resolutely and went over to her closet to pick out a pair of shoes.

"Oh." Melissa remembered. "I won. I'm the new president of the student council."

"Congratulations! I'm proud of you! You're going to be a great president!"

"I hope so!"

The sudden loud peal of the doorbell caused them both to start.

"That's probably Lee," Melissa said. "I'd better go let him in. Don't worry, I won't be home late—maybe I'll even be back before you!" she couldn't resist adding slyly. Grabbing her books from the foyer table, she ran to the door.

"Have a good time, Madam President!" her mother called after her.

"All set?" Lee asked, stretching out his hand to draw her closer to him.

"All set!" answered Melissa.

And she was. For whatever the future held.

First Love from Silhouette

COMING NEXT MONTH

JOURNEY'S END
Becky Stuart
A Kellogg and Carey Story!
In an attempt to determine the identity of a dead man,
Kellogg and Carey learn something about the nature
of love.

FREE SPIRIT
Katrina West
To Kara's dismay, her mom married a disk jockey and
they all moved into a haunted house. Worse yet, her
boyfriend appeared to be more interested in chasing the
ghost than in chasing Kara.

SUGAR 'N' SPICE
Janice Harrell
Now that Fran had achieved her heart's desire and was
actually dating dreamboat Steve, why was she bored out
of her squash?

THE OTHER LANGLEY GIRL
Joyce McGill
For years Beth's pretty and popular older sister had been
her role model. How could Beth cope with the discovery
that her sister was not quite as perfect as she had
imagined?

AVAILABLE THIS MONTH

**THE PHANTOM
SKATEBOARD**
Elaine Harper

ONE IN A MILLION
Kathryn Makris

A CIVIL WAR
Beverly Sommers

FORTUNE'S CHILD
Cheryl Zach